PUFFIN BOOKS

TALES FROM BEYOND THE RAINBOW

TALES FROM BEYOND THE RAINBOW

Collected and adapted by

PETE JORDI WOOD

PUFFIN CLASSICS

PUFFIN BOOKS

UK | USA | Canada | Ireland | Australia
India | New Zealand | South Africa

Puffin Books is part of the Penguin Random House group of companies
whose addresses can be found at global.penguinrandomhouse.com

www.penguin.co.uk
www.puffin.co.uk
www.ladybird.co.uk

Penguin Random House UK

First published 2023
This edition published 2024

001

Typeset by Jouve (UK), Milton Keynes
Printed and bound in Great Britain by Clays Ltd, Elcograf S.p.A.

The authorized representative in the EEA is Penguin Random House Ireland,
Morrison Chambers, 32 Nassau Street, Dublin D02 YH68

A CIP catalogue record for this book is available from the British Library

ISBN: 978–0–241–54543–0

All correspondence to:
Puffin Books
Penguin Random House Children's
One Embassy Gardens, 8 Viaduct Gardens, London SW11 7BW

MIX
Paper | Supporting responsible forestry
FSC www.fsc.org FSC® C018179

Penguin Random House is committed to a sustainable future for our business, our readers and our planet. This book is made from Forest Stewardship Council® certified paper.

For the LGBTQ+ storytellers of the past:
may your tales continue to be told.

CONTENTS

INTRODUCTION

Folklore is all around you. It is hidden in the memes you send to friends on your phone, and the graffiti you find on toilet walls. It is in the ghost stories you whisper beside campfires, and the zany conspiracy theories you read on social media. Folklore is the traditional, informal culture we pick up through word of mouth, gossip and general observations of the world around us. We seldom know who the original creator of a piece of folklore was (or even where and when it came into existence), but somehow, from its very inception, it belongs to us all.

Unlike myths and legends, which usually concern themselves with the deeds of powerful gods and goddesses or kings and queens, folk tales generally focus on people like you and me – the ordinary folk. Even in stories about princes, the hero is usually stripped of their royal title and has to live as 'one of us' for a time. Folk tales are *our* tales.

Folklore also includes the fairy tales we tell one another, sometimes as quietly as a bedtime story, or as loudly as a movie on the big screen. Fairy tales are so captivating that they have become probably the most popular genre of folklore. They add sparkle to ordinary life and, through the power of our imagination, enable us to go on extraordinary adventures, meet magical creatures and accomplish spectacular things.

Some fairy tales date back centuries and have, over their long lifetimes, shape-shifted into many different forms. As merchants, migrants and sailors travelled around the globe, the folk and fairy tales of their home countries and cultures journeyed with them. We ensured the preservation of our fairy tales by passing down these stories from one generation to the next. We were all storytellers.

The term 'folklore' was introduced by William John Thoms in 1846 because he feared that our storytelling heritage was being lost. As cities grew during the Industrial Revolution, and the printing press created a world full of books, more and more people were learning to read. This meant they were *telling* stories – literally speaking them out loud – less often, and some tales were no longer being passed on at all.

Thoms called on people to start writing down the folk tales of the world before they were lost. As a British man, his call went out from London, through Europe and off to the far corners of the British Empire. He was answered by hundreds of people. These self-named 'folklorists' were well-meaning, passionate and committed. What they weren't, unfortunately, was diverse.

The folklorists of the late nineteenth and early twentieth centuries were overwhelmingly male, white, able-bodied, rich and, from what we know, cisgender. There *were* some female folklorists, and some who were working class, people of colour, disabled and whose gender identity or sexuality is unknown, but these examples are rare. Inevitably, the biases and privilege of the majority of folklorists influenced their work.

When collecting stories from different ethnic groups, many folklorists tried to write down the tales exactly as they were told. But this didn't always work, and some collections included degrading comments about the people from whom they had sourced stories, reflecting the grim reality of nineteenth-century racism.

Growing up in a single-parent family with no siblings, books – particularly fairy tales – were my whole world. But I longed to see myself represented in the stories I loved so much, to discover someone like me in those pages who meets his Prince Charming, or goes on a magical adventure and is rewarded with a happy-ever-after. And so, as an adult, like those who heeded Thoms's call in 1846, I set off on a quest to find some fairy tales – ones that featured people like me. The result is the anthology you are holding right now.

Scouring folklore collections from around the world, I've created a collection of my favourite stories featuring positive portrayals of LGBTQ+ people: stories about love in its many forms, transformation, identity and gender, hope, survival and living life as your true self. At the end of this book you will find an 'About the Tales' appendix with information about each tale, their sources and origins, and the reasoning behind any changes I have made, along with suggested reading that might interest you if you want to research them more, or write your own adaptations through *your* unique lens.

And what of my lens? Well, I'm gay, non-binary, I have a disability, and at the time of writing I live in social housing, so I am writing as a relatively marginalized voice in society. But I'm also white and Western, and I acknowledge my privilege. From the start of this project, I've been keen not to repeat the mistakes of the past, and instead seek a way of collecting stories from around the world without being culturally insensitive and appropriative, whilst at the same time expanding our knowledge of, and access to, these ancient, awesome tales. For any mistakes or missteps I have made, forgive me, for I am still learning. My goal has been to enable these stories to be shared, so that young LGBTQ+ people can see themselves represented in ways in which I never saw myself as a child.

In the past, many stories about gender have not treated trans and non-binary people kindly, with preoccupations surrounding our bodies rather than our experiences and our lives. Many fairy tales are problematic in their presentation of LGBTQ+ characters who experience sudden magical gender transformations, or violence and death at the hands of others. However, I have found that many of these tales are also ripe for reclamation and reinterpretation.

Therefore, in adapting the stories, I've tried to stick as closely as possible to the original narratives, while updating the tales for contemporary readers through sensitivity to the depiction of different genders and identities and their pronoun choices, and with an emphasis on the overall positive portrayal of LGBTQ+ characters. I have worked with authenticity readers from around the world, whose insight and expertise have immeasurably improved and enriched the stories, as has the work of the wonderful illustrators, many of them from the LGBTQ+ community, all of them sharing a heritage with the culture from which the story they have illustrated has been drawn.

Limits of space have restricted this collection to ten stories, but I hope that, in the future, more collections like this will exist, to preserve and explore our collective LGBTQ+ folklore, offering representation to those whose identities it has not been possible to include here. All of us are unique. How we live our lives, how we feel within our bodies, and how we experience love, varies from one person to the next. Our myriad experiences – of pain, happiness, dysphoria and euphoria – are so deeply personal that at times I have wondered if I should even be attempting to write about any of these things at all.

However, if history tells us one thing, it's that

anyone can be a folklorist – and that includes you. Many folk-tale collections written in the nineteenth and early twentieth centuries are now available to view online for free. Who knows what you might find in those pages, the forgotten fairy tales of our past? Re-examine them through *your* eyes and see if there are more examples of LGBTQ+ characters in those tales that history has overlooked, more representations of disabled characters, or further instances of people of colour, taking the reins of their tales. Maybe the story of your own experience or identity is out there, waiting to be found and shared once more, by you.

Although retellings of classic fairy tales with an LGBTQ+ spin have been popular for some time, traditional folk tales about LGBTQ+ people are not a contemporary invention. They exist in every corner of the globe. And their continued existence is more important than ever in our world right now because they prove something vital – that LGBTQ+ people have not always been vilified by society but celebrated as the heroes, sheroes, theyroes and queeroes of their own stories, since time immemorial.

THE GIRL IN THE MARKET

Illustrated by

Mario Hounkanrin

A long time ago in the Dahomey Kingdom, many years before the country of Benin was founded, there stood a vast city in the western savannah. Its walls stretched one hundred miles, each brick cast in bronze.

The city was ruled by the young King Dadase, who took the throne when he was just eighteen, upon the death of his father. His days were now filled with public engagements and meetings with his advisors, amidst endless schooling from his strict teachers. His lessons were held in a tower that overlooked the city, and during them Dadase often found himself staring out of the windows into the streets, where boys and girls his own age smiled and joked together. Dadase wished he could join them, just for a day, to have some fun and forget the responsibility he had inherited with his title.

And so one morning Dadase decided to venture out beyond the palace gates in disguise. He had noticed that when the cook came to work he brought with him a beige robe into which he changed to pray. So Dadase removed his fine jewellery and went to the kitchens in search of it.

The cook was outside in the courtyard, busying himself plucking a chicken. Dadase found the robe neatly folded on a shelf, and hurriedly removed his elegant embroidered tunic. Pulling the robe over his head, he stared at his reflection in one of the silver dishes and smiled; he looked no longer like a king but an ordinary man. Bowing his head, and careful not to look the guards in the eye, Dadase quietly left the palace and stepped barefoot into the dusty streets of the world beyond.

He headed to the market, which he had long yearned to visit. Within a labyrinth of alleyways, its traders hawked their treasures. Dadase breathed in the sweet scents of this wondrous place. Laid out before him were pyramids of pineapples and baskets of cashews, yams and corn. An old man roasted chicken on a spit as a queue of customers licked their lips in anticipation of their first bite.

Of course, Dadase was no stranger to the rich and varied flavours of his kingdom. Every evening he dined on the very finest cuts of meat and the freshest vegetables and spices that the cook had gathered for his meal. But he had never set foot in the market himself. As Dadase turned a corner and saw a girl in the market, he immediately fell in love with her.

Many great rulers had brought their daughters to the kingdom in the hope that Dadase would take one of them as his wife. He had met some of the most beautiful women in the world, dressed in the most splendid clothes, their hands and necks heavy with the weight of jewels. And yet the girl in the market, who had no rings on her fingers and not a single thread of silk in her head-scarf, had qualities no other possessed: a sparkle in her eyes, a smile that illuminated the shady corner in which she sat and a laugh that made him laugh too . . . for the first time in forever.

The girl, the same age as Dadase, sat upon a step, her legs crossed in front of her as she called to passers-by to sample her grandmother's delicious peanut sauce. After just a spoonful, her customers eagerly bought jars to take home with them.

As Dadase turned a corner and saw a girl in the market, he immediately fell in love with her.

Dadase approached the girl and placed some gold coins at her feet, offering to buy every single jar she had brought to market. The girl beamed, delighted by such a display of generosity. As she carefully placed the jars in a cotton sack and handed them to him, Dadase became overwhelmed with emotion and could not help but declare his love.

'I am your king, but today I stand before you as an ordinary man,' said Dadase, taking the girl's hands in his. 'And, upon finding you, I do not wish to let you go. Do me the honour of becoming my bride, and return with me to the palace so I might look upon your face every day.'

The crowd gasped. No one could have imagined that their king would walk amongst them. And no one could have foreseen that of all the girls in the market he might fall in love with this one in particular. The other traders, who had seen the girl come to market with her grandmother for many years, knew her history. They could remember the day she was born, and how her father had excitedly told everyone that his family had welcomed a son. They knew the name she was first given, though few were so disrespectful as to call her by it now.

Dausi was shocked by the young king's proposal too. Dadase was extremely handsome, even dressed in a simple robe, and his honest declaration of love had moved her deeply. Staring into his longing eyes, she had not the heart to reject his offer, nor the wish to – for she knew that she loved him too.

However, Dausi wanted to be sure that the king would love her despite her past, and so she asked him to sit with her, and told him her story. As her tale drew to a close, she looked away, scared to meet his gaze in case he should reject her.

But Dadase simply repeated his question.

'Will you marry me?'

'Yes,' said Dausi, beaming.

And, with that, Dadase and the poor girl from the market walked back to the palace. Dausi looked down at her hand, which the king held so tightly, and felt a great wave of happiness flood her body, from her fingertips to the depths of her heart.

***

During her first few weeks in the palace, every day seemed like a dream. So smitten was Dadase that he showered Dausi with gifts and affection. The king insisted his tailors be at Dausi's disposal whenever she wished, and each day she rose excited to discover a beautiful new dress folded neatly on her bed to wear. There were women who braided her hair, and in their company, as they shared their stories, Dausi felt a sense of sisterhood unlike any she'd known before.

However, when Dausi had agreed to marry the king, she had not fully considered how the act would change her life. For not only would she become his bride but she'd become the kingdom's queen. Although the thought of such a thing filled her with pride, she also worried that there might be some who would not accept her taking this title.

Dausi's concerns were sadly founded in truth. Some in the palace had noticed that Dausi was distracting Dadase from his duties as king. One of them was Aluba, an ambitious woman who had long yearned to be Dadase's bride herself. Her mother had served as an advisor to Dadase's father, and her grandmother to his grandfather. She had noticed that Dadase had paid less attention to her advice since Dausi had arrived at the palace, and she was very jealous.

One of the things Aluba loved most was gossip, and she liked nothing more than to help a rumour take flight. So when she learned that some in the palace were whispering secrets about Dausi and her past, Aluba saw an opportunity to regain her influence over the king.

'Get out of my way!' she yelled at a young maid, pushing past her in her haste to reach the king's chambers. Aluba couldn't wait to tell the king and his courtiers about Dausi's secret past. She believed that Dadase's favour would fall once more upon her, and she would be rewarded handsomely for helping to expel a traitor from his inner circle.

Aluba found the king sat upon his throne reading, and hurried to his side.

'Dausi is a man!' she exclaimed.

But Dadase looked upon her with disdain, annoyed that Aluba had interrupted his peace.

'Aluba, you have been in my life for longer than I can remember,' said the king, 'but you cannot remain by my side if you say such venomous things.'

'But I speak the truth!' said Aluba, desperate that the king believed her.

'The only truth is that Dausi is a woman,' said the king. 'We have no secrets between us, and she has told me her story. A story which is not yours, only hers, to share.'

Aluba left the room. She returned to her quarters and wept, and after some time rage took hold of her soul. As the stars passed overhead, she stared at the ceiling, plotting ways to stop Dausi from being crowned queen, until eventually she landed on a plan to drive her away forever.

The next day, Aluba visited Dausi early with an offering of flowers.

'Today the women go to the spring to make offerings to the fetishes,' she announced. 'Will you sit at the gates of the palace with me and watch them pass? It is quite the spectacle. I have fresh melons for us to enjoy while we watch.'

Dausi knew well the custom of which Aluba spoke. Their bodies anointed with fat, their necks and arms dusted with àtíkè powder, hundreds of women from the city would parade to the river to honour the fetishes – beautiful statues depicting the different spirits of the land. The women wore the most beautiful pearl belts and bracelets, which caught the light of the sun.

For much of the afternoon, Aluba and Dausi ate and talked and laughed together. Dausi was pleased to have found another woman in the palace to whom she felt she could open her heart.

'As a child, I often wondered what it would feel like to walk amongst them,' said Dausi softly as they watched the procession pass by, 'and I dreamt one day I might.'

Aluba said nothing. Instead, she grinned, because she knew that Dausi now trusted her and would listen to her, whatever she had to say.

In the weeks that followed, Aluba made Dausi's life a misery. When Dausi asked her for her opinion on the clothes she planned to wear for her wedding, Aluba told her they did not suit her. When introducing Dausi to others, Aluba told them how Dausi had been born poor, and corrected Dausi when she did or said things outside of palace etiquette. Though Aluba presented her advice as kindness, she knew that it would cause Dausi humiliation.

And it did. Dausi soon began to question whether she could ever fit in within this royal world, and if she even deserved to be there. She was, after all, just the girl from the market – could she really become the queen that everybody wanted? A queen who walked a certain way and spoke of royal matters with grace and poise?

Worst of all, although she was careful not to do so in front of the king, time and time again Aluba pretended to forget Dausi's name, and instead referred to her by the name she had been given at birth. When Dausi asked her politely to use her chosen name instead, Aluba would apologize loudly, using the wrong name again, so that everyone around them would hear.

Aluba's words stung like a scorpion's tail, and every time Dausi heard them, a little of her happiness drained away. She grew more anxious about the wedding, worried what the people of the kingdom would think of her when they saw her crowned at Dadase's side. At night, she could not sleep. For many years Dausi had felt at peace, but now, slowly, from somewhere within her, the fear that had once occupied her thoughts returned like a deep and endless heartbreak.

On the eve of her wedding, as the palace slumbered, Dausi sneaked to the kitchens, just as Dadase had done on the day they met. Taking care not to wake anyone, she boiled some cornmeal and carefully rolled it into pellets. After storing them in a calabash and checking the courtyard was clear, she pulled a shawl over her head and ventured into the night.

For Dadase, leaving the palace in disguise had been an easy task. The dogs that guarded each of its forty gates knew his scent and had been trained since pups to always let him pass. But Dausi knew that they would bark if she approached them, and alert the sleeping guards of her escape.

Fortunately, her plan worked. One by one, the dogs at each gate wolfed down the cornmeal she fed them, distracted long enough for her to pass in silence. Dausi eventually found herself back in the dusty city streets and, knowing them well, fled through the back alleys at such speed that very soon she had reached the familiar world of the market again.

In the dead of night, the market was a different place. Gone were its sights and scents and the chatter of a thousand voices. Dausi sat in the dirt at the spot she'd always taken to sell her peanut sauce. She paused there for a moment, looking back at the distant spires of the palace far behind her.

Dausi remembered looking up at Dadase for the first time, right here, into eyes that looked upon her in a way no others had – not with curiosity or confusion but love. She knew she should be happy, but that felt impossible. She knew she could be queen – and yet Aluba, and who knew how many others, still looked at her with suspicion and fear in their hearts.

And so Dausi stood again, and bravely ventured through the city gates into the savannah and its many dangers. Many before her had ventured there, into an unknown world of magic and wondrous things. Some returned transformed by their experience, whilst others were never seen again. Dausi wondered if she too might change and if such a wish could be granted by the spirits of the wilderness. But, ultimately, she did not know where she was going, nor cared much what became of her.

***

In the early hours of the next morning, before the sun had risen, Dadase woke as he always did – eager to spend time with Dausi. He dressed and hurried to her chamber, but upon arriving there he was surprised to find Aluba instead.

'Your Grace,' said Aluba, trying to contain her glee, 'Dausi has run away. Perhaps she feared she would never be accepted as your queen. What joyous day, now she has gone, for you are free to take another as your bride.'

But to Aluba's surprise Dadase fell to his knees and cried out. His voice carried across the city, and all could hear his pain. But even the dry Harmattan wind could not deliver it to Dausi, now so very far away.

Dausi had journeyed many miles, following the path of the moon. She had waded in the mangroves and escaped the hippo's tusks. She had crossed the fallow fields through the smoke of its burning brush. She had passed through the sacred forests where the monkeys had screamed at her to leave. Finally, as the skies turned overcast and rain began to fall, she sought shelter under a baobab tree and looked out across the wilderness that stretched to the horizon. There, antelopes grazed, unaware that lions were circling them.

But the antelopes were not alone in being hunted. Startled by the snap of a branch, Dausi turned to see two yellow eyes staring back at her from the thorny scrub. Hyena bared his teeth and growled. But, to his surprise, Dausi simply shrugged, and stared at the ground.

'Hyena,' she said, 'I am very unhappy. Carry me away.'

Hyena could see from her hopeless eyes that Dausi told the truth, and so instead of pouncing on his prey, he turned away. But no sooner had he left than another beast arrived. Panther was hungry and had sensed Dausi from afar. Dausi sighed and buried her head in her arms.

'Panther,' she said, 'I am very unhappy. Carry me away.'

Panther shook his head. He could see from her desperate plea that Dausi told the truth, and no meal was worth eating that felt no worth in itself.

As Panther left, Dausi looked up, a shadow falling upon her. A figure stood tall by the baobab tree; his hand reached out towards her. Dausi recognized him at once.

'Death,' she whispered, exhausted, 'I am very unhappy. Carry me away.'

But Death did not strike her down. Instead, he sat with her.

'Tell me, girl, what troubles you?' he said.

'I cannot find the words,' Dausi replied.

'Try if you can,' Death encouraged her.

Dausi stared blankly into the distance.

'I fear that others will never see me as I see myself,' she said eventually.

Death sighed.

'Then let me remind you what they see,' he said, and covered her eyes with his palms.

A gust of wind suddenly blew across the savannah and leaves fell from the tree. The world was plunged into darkness, and for a moment Dausi could not feel the ground beneath her. Then, slowly, her eyes adjusted and she saw someone ahead, looking back at her, smiling; she was sat upon the ground, surrounded by bottles of peanut sauce. She was the girl in the market.

In that moment, Dausi saw how Dadase must have seen her the day they met, and how she had looked back at him, a sparkle in her eyes. And, like Dadase had done, Dausi felt a sudden warmth that spread through every fibre of her being, as love swelled in her heart.

Death removed his hands, and Dausi opened her eyes. The sun was rising, and the first thing she saw was her shadow, cast upon the trunk of the baobab tree. She stared at her silhouette and noticed for the first time how it pleased her, her long hair flickering in the breeze.

'What did you see?' asked Death.

'A woman who I love,' said Dausi. 'And a queen.'

***

Back in the city, Aluba had decided not to let the preparations for the royal wedding go to waste. She saw an opportunity to impress the king, and commanded that the feast should go ahead in his honour, thinking that perhaps he'd take her as his bride instead. She marched around the palace, barking orders to the servants, many of whom had been working since before dawn.

Then she heard something that deeply troubled her: a singing voice that drifted through the palace corridors. Aluba instantly recognized that it belonged to Dausi. Following the song, she arrived at Dausi's chamber where she discovered Dausi wrapping a long skirt around her waist.

'But I thought you ran away!' said Aluba.

'Why would I do so,' replied Dausi, 'when I am the happiest I've ever been?'

Aluba stared at her, horrified. There was nothing she could say that could extinguish Dausi's joy, which radiated from her so brightly. Dausi had ignored Aluba's advice and now stood before her in the clothes she'd picked to wear for the wedding, and her beauty could not be denied.

At that moment, Dadase, who had also heard Dausi's voice, ran into the room.

'I thought you were gone,' said the king, embracing her with tears in his eyes.

Looking on, Aluba stamped her feet, livid.

'You will never be my queen, you fraud!' she roared, her blood boiling with hate. Her heart beat fast, her eyes turned red, and her fists clenched so tight that her nails pierced her skin.

'Dear Aluba,' said Dausi calmly, 'please sit down; you don't look well.'

But Aluba was so angry that no one could restrain her. The king's guards ran into the room and tried to hold her back. But still she raged and swore and screamed all manner of terrible things, until she felt the room begin to spin about her. Then she stopped, and saw Dausi staring back at her, her mouth agape. She looked at the guards and their shocked faces. But what hurt her most of all was the disappointment in Dadase's eyes. Aluba attempted to regain her composure as the king approached her cautiously.

'It is you who are the fraud,' he said. 'For you pretended to be Dausi's friend, and now the truth has been exposed.'

The king ordered his guards to carry Aluba away until her rage had calmed. As she sat inside a prison cell, alone with her regrets, thc rest of the palace came together to celebrate Dadase and Dausi's wedding. The girl from the market took her place at the king's side, and the whole city feasted for three days. And they reigned for many years together, and Dausi became the most beloved of queens.

Double-Flower Temple

Illustrated by

Xin Tang

During the reign of the Yongzheng Emperor, somewhere in the north-east of China, near the great city of Guilin, there lived a student called Cai. Each day he would wander from his home through the streets, smiling at passers-by. The air was filled with the sweet fragrance of the osmanthus trees that grew all around the neighbourhood, ushering in the season of spring. He was handsome and polite, and well liked by his community, so everyone smiled back at him.

Cai loved the theatre, and whenever he had enough money he would go to watch plays. In the darkness of the auditorium, he would lose himself in the stories told onstage. Through them, he journeyed to imagined worlds far beyond Guilin, and witnessed heroes fall in love, embark on adventures and fight gruesome beasts.

However, one day Cai woke from a daydream only to find himself in another. Whilst watching a play he felt something brush his arm. Upon looking down, he saw it was a hand, belonging to the young man who was seated next to him. Initially he was annoyed that his attention had been interrupted, but when he turned to see the young man's face he immediately fell in love with him.

'My name is Zixin,' the young man whispered, bowing his head a little, and took Cai's hand in his. For the rest of the performance they sat in the darkness together, glancing shyly at each other whenever they believed the other was looking away.

After the play, Cai and Zixin walked together along the River Li and talked for hours. When Zixin's hat blew away in the wind, Cai ran to retrieve it for him, and they laughed until they cried like the oldest of friends. Zixin revealed that he was also from Guilin, from a wealthy family, and that he aspired to be a student like Cai too.

As the sun began to set, they arrived at a tavern called Apricot Blossom Village, named after the beautiful trees surrounding it. After drinking until the early hours, Cai took Zixin's hand in his once again, and they took an oath of eternal loyalty to each other. But they were so happy that they did not notice another man in the tavern glaring at them from afar . . .

From that day onwards, Cai and Zixin were inseparable. Every weekend they travelled together to and from the city. They both loved to explore the food of the city, sharing plates and offering each other bites of their favourite dishes. They made an extremely attractive couple, both disregarding the masculine fashions of the time, and instead dressing as they felt comfortable: their faces shaved, their clothes cut in elegant, feminine styles. As they walked through the city together, some would point and stare, but Cai and Zixin were so happy to be in one another's company that they did not care to notice.

Unfortunately, Wang Tu'er did not like to be ignored. Not much older than Cai and Zixin, he was the man who had glared at them from the shadows. From afar he had watched as Cai and Zixin's friendship deepened and witnessed their love bloom like the apricot blossom beyond the tavern's walls. Although the boys smiled at Wang and always greeted him whenever they saw him, Wang had grown to hate them, even though he did not understand why. All Wang knew was that seeing them so happy together disgusted him, and he wanted to extinguish their flame.

And so, one night, as Cai and Zixin left the tavern and walked along the riverbank, Wang burst from the bushes and attacked them, pushing them both into the swirling currents of the river, which drew them down into the depths.

A few days later, Cai's and Zixin's devastated parents reported them missing. The bodies of the young lovers were soon discovered washed up on the riverbank, their hands clasped together just as on the night they'd met.

Wang attempted to flee the city, but witnesses from the tavern confirmed to the police that he had long hated the boys. Wang eventually confessed to their murders, a crime for which he was executed.

In the months that followed, the city of Guilin seemed a less happy place. Many missed the sight of the two young men walking the streets hand in hand, their laughter echoing through the alleyways. The tavern was silent with the grief of those who had and hadn't known them well. Cai and Zixin had been the most courteous and faithful young men, and everyone mourned that they had been lost too soon.

And so, as a mark of respect, the community decided to build a temple in their honour. The Double-Flower Temple was so called because when locals came to make offerings to the young lovers, they would bring branches of apricot blossoms, like those found outside the tavern where Cai and Zixin had often met. As the years turned over, the Double-Flower Temple became one of the city's most popular shrines. For whoever went there to burn incense and make offerings to Cai and Zixin discovered that their prayers were soon answered.

Ten years after their deaths, Liu Big Beard, the county magistrate, came to inspect the temple himself. He had heard of its reputation as the site of many miracles, and was curious about the story behind it. But when some of the locals told him the story of Cai and Zixin he was enraged. Those old enough to remember recognized his disgust – the very same as Wang's.

'This is a temple for deviants!' he cried. 'Why should good, honest people worship two such wicked young men?'

To the dismay of the people, Liu immediately ordered the local constable to destroy the temple and raze it to the ground.

However, that night Liu had a terrifying nightmare. He dreamt that two young men came to his room. Although he had never met them, he recognized them immediately from the paintings in the Double-Flower Temple. Both handsome, their hands clasped together, they were unmistakably the ghosts of Cai and Zixin. The ghosts grabbed Liu's beard, but when he tried to scream no sound left his lips. Instead, he froze and stared at the eyes of the ghosts as they stared back into his.

But Cai and Zixin were not violent, and they did not wish to scare Liu out of his wits. They knew that it is only education, not fear, that can change a person's point of view. And so, sitting at the end of Liu's bed, they explained that his hatred of them was no more rational than Wang's had been. Why did he care what clothes they wore in public, or what loving words they said to each other in private?

'Besides, who are you to judge whether we were wicked or not?' they said. 'We did no harm and yet we were murdered. You have taken bribes to turn a blind eye to crimes, and yet you live.'

Liu was astonished that the ghosts knew his deepest secret.

'Are you . . . are you going to kill me?' asked the magistrate, trembling.

Both handsome, their hands clasped, they were unmistakably the ghosts of Cai and Zixin.

Cai and Zixin shook their heads.

'Your judgement will come not from our hands,' said the ghosts, twisting the hair of Liu's beard round a stick. 'One day you will understand.'

With that, they disappeared.

The next morning, Liu went back to the Double-Flower Temple, where a number of locals had gathered to protest against its destruction. Liu stared at the building, and, although he could recognize its beauty, he still did not believe it should be allowed to stand.

As the constable approached him, Liu bowed respectfully – and was surprised when the constable bound his hands with ropes.

'I am here to arrest you,' said the constable, 'for it has come to light that you have taken bribes. I needn't tell you, for you are the magistrate, that the punishment for such a crime is death by hanging.'

Only then did Liu understand that the ghosts had come to warn him, and that the twisted beard was a prophecy of a noose round his neck. In one last attempt to save his life, he told the constable and everyone present that he'd had a change of heart, but he was nevertheless carried off to prison.

The people of the city appealed to the new magistrate, who decided that the Double-Flower Temple would not be destroyed, after all. And ever since, if you go there, and listen very carefully, you can still hear those ghost boys laughing together and talking all night long.

The Falcon in the Garden

Illustrated by

Zat Vornik

Far beyond the Ural Mountains, in a kingdom long forgotten, there once was a priest who lived with his daughter. Vasilisa Vasilyevna was a pretty girl, with the fairest blonde hair that curled around her ears and eyes as green as a meadow in spring. Their home was humble, next to the church in which the priest served God and his congregation. The priest was beloved by his community, and many attended his services to worship. His humorous and hopeful sermons made life in the kingdom a little brighter, and his warm and loving nature made everyone who entered the church feel welcome.

King Barkhat, on the other hand, was not quite so popular a man. Like his father and grandfather before him, he ruled his people with an iron fist. The young king valued tradition and insisted that his subjects wear simple clothes or else be thrown into prison. He disliked bright colours and ordered his builders to construct buildings in plain stone, painted only in black and white. In the whole kingdom, barely a handful of colourful buildings, too important to be torn down, remained. When he looked out upon the city from his palace windows, the king considered the priest's church, with its striking striped turrets in a spectrum of rainbow tones, a particularly ugly and unwelcome eyesore.

As Vasilisa grew up, she began to question the many regulations King Barkhat had imposed upon his people. Every rule the king had set,

Vasilisa yearned to break. She knew from an early age that she did not want to behave as the king instructed – nor could she, even if she had so desired. The king dictated that boys should behave very differently from girls, and that each should know his or her place.

And so the boys in the kingdom wore trousers and caps, and the girls wore dresses and bonnets. The boys were taught to hunt, to ride horses and to fire rifles. The girls were taught to sew, to cook and to clean. Should anyone rebel against the rules, they were thrown in prison until they could prove they were willing to conform. But mostly those who disappeared vanished forever.

Seeing the world in shades of black and white, the king was unable to perceive the range of colours that existed alongside them and in between. He believed that women and men looked a certain way, and did certain things, and each served a different purpose, and that was frankly that.

Vasilisa felt in every fibre of her being that to become the sort of person the king ordered her to be was not her destiny. She gathered various unclaimed treasures found in the church and its surrounding streets: a blue feathered cap left in a pew, a soldier's rifle dropped beside a forest stream, some trousers blown from a washing-line by a breeze, and an orphaned horse with a chestnut mane that had strayed too far from home.

When no one was looking, Vasilisa would tuck her hair into her cap, pull on her trousers and, looking like any other boy her age, strap her rifle to her side, mount her horse and ride through the countryside, hunting for rabbits. She became so skilled that she and her father ate well every night. She did not hide this side of herself from her father. Although he worried that she might be punished, he knew in his heart that his daughter should be whoever she wanted to be.

As Vasilisa grew older, she abandoned her dresses altogether and no longer went out in public as Vasilisa but instead as her true self: a young man called Vasily. He competed in horseback races and won, drinking vodka afterwards in the taverns to celebrate.

For a long time, Vasily enjoyed his life and was accepted amongst the community without question. But all this was to change when one day the jealous king decided to attend a mass at the church to see why it was so popular with the city's population.

As he left afterwards, the king saw Vasily galloping home from his daily hunting trip to the forests, six rabbits slung at his side. Vasily hurried into the priest's cottage to prepare his father's dinner.

The king's brief glimpse of the handsome hunter had left him completely enchanted.

'Who was that young man?' he asked his servant.

The king liked to surround himself with those who thought the same way as he did, and this servant was no exception; for many years he had followed the king as his most loyal disciple. He had heard of Vasily's story, and it had made him quite uncomfortable, so he was quick to reveal it to the king.

'Your Majesty, that boy was once a girl,' he replied. 'Vasilisa Vasilyevna, the daughter of the priest. But now they call him Vasily instead.'

Confused, the king returned to the palace, but he could not get Vasily out of his head. Late that night, he wrote a letter to the priest, inviting his son to dinner at the palace. As the king waited for a response, he paced impatiently in the courtyard, where the old witch and hermit Taisiya lived in an old barrel turned on its side.

'Wise witch,' said the king, 'I have seen a young man, but my servant says he is a girl. How do I determine whether he be Vasily, or she be Vasilisa?'

Two little eyes blinked from the shadows of the barrel. Emerging from it, Taisiya grinned, showing the king her yellow teeth.

'Hang up an embroidery frame upon the wall,' she said, raising a finger in the air decisively, 'and beside it hang a gun. If she is Vasilisa Vasilyevna, she will first notice the frame. But if he is Vasily Vasilyevich, the weapon will draw his attention instead.'

With that, the witch returned to the barrel, just as the king's messenger returned: Vasily had accepted the offer and would attend a dinner with the king at the palace the very next day.

The king wanted to impress Vasily, so he prepared a most delicious feast. The magnificent spread included golden plates of blinis, bowls of steaming stroganoff, and hot, sweet syrniki pancakes and fresh berries. Just as the witch had suggested, the palace servants hung an embroidery hoop upon the wall to the right of the king's seat at the table, and to his left they hung a gun.

Vasily soon arrived, wearing his favourite cap, and greeted King Barkhat graciously. Together they entered the palace and walked through the long corridors to the impressive dining hall, where the king offered Vasily a seat at his table. As Vasily dug into the tasty treats in front of him, the king waited for him to look up and see which item upon the wall would catch his attention first.

Eventually, Vasily looked up from his plate and smiled at the king, his eyes drifting to the wall. They fell first upon the frame, but to the king's surprise Vasily said: 'Does the king love to embroider? For you hang hoops upon your walls. It is a surprise to see such things in the home of a man. In my father's house there is nothing of the kind.'

With that, Vasily stood, thanked the king for the meal and left the palace for home. Confused,

King Barkhat stared up at the embroidery hoop and the gun, none the wiser as to whether his guest was Vasily or Vasilisa.

Unable to sleep that night, the king sent another letter, again inviting Vasily to the palace for dinner. A date was set, and Vasily and the king soon found themselves once again in the grand dining hall with a feast in front of them.

This time, the old witch had instructed the king to carry out a different plan. He ordered his cook to prepare a dish of kasha, but to stuff the creamy porridge with pearls and serve it at the end of the feast.

'If the youth is truly Vasilisa Vasilyevna,' Taisiya explained, 'she will place the pearls in a neat pile on the table. But if he is Vasily Vasilyevich, he will throw them under the table without hesitation.'

And so, as the kasha was served, the king stared at Vasily intently to see what he would do. As

Vasily chewed and his teeth struck a pearl, he spat it from his mouth to the floor.

'What sort of kasha is this?' said Vasily with surprise. 'In my father's house, we have not one single piece of jewellery, but in yours it's everywhere. Does the king love jewellery so much he must even have it in his food?'

He stood abruptly, thanked the king for the meal and bade him farewell once again.

Astonished, the king returned to his chamber, unable still to decide whether his guest was Vasily or Vasilisa. With each test, his curiosity had deepened, until knowing the answer to his question had become his greatest obsession.

The king returned to the courtyard to seek the witch's guidance. Two little eyes blinked from her barrel, and she emerged with her final instructions.

'Invite the youth to visit the bathhouse where the men sit in steam,' said the witch. 'For if she is

Astonished, the king returned to his chamber, unable still to decide whether his guest was Vasily or Vasilisa.

Vasilisa Vasilyevna she will refuse to join you. But if he is Vasily Vasilyevich he will accompany you there.'

The king's messenger delivered the invitation to Vasily to join the king once more for dinner. Vasily accepted and soon found himself at the king's dinner table, tucking into another feast of fine foods. As the meal concluded, the king turned to Vasily and asked if he wished to join him for a visit to the bathhouse.

'Certainly, Your Majesty,' replied Vasily promptly. 'For I have not bathed in a long time and would like to very much.'

And so the king and Vasily went to the bathhouse. The king undressed in his private changing room, but in order to impress Vasily he had worn many layers of his most elegant black robes, which took him a while to remove. By the time the king was ready to bathe, Vasily had already taken his bath and dressed again. Annoyed, King Barkhat emerged, red-faced from both the steam and his embarrassment, to find a servant waiting for him with a note from Vasily.

Ah, King Barkhat, it read, *raven that you are, you cannot surprise a falcon in a garden. For I am neither he nor she but all the colours in between.*

That was the last time Vasily accepted an invitation to dinner with the king. Instead, they rode away from the kingdom forever and experienced many adventures and loves. Meanwhile, King Barkhat lived out the rest of his days alone, in his city of black and white, because that was all he was able to see.

The Spinners and the Sorcerer

Illustrated by

Sophia Watts

A long time ago there lived a wicked sorcerer who practised the most sinister magical arts. He lived in a house hidden away in the dark heart of the forest and only came out when the moon was full, venturing into the nearby town disguised as a poor beggar. Travelling from door to door, he carried a large basket on his back, in which he kept the food he was given. Over the years, many pretty girls from the town had disappeared, but the townsfolk were baffled, for no one knew where they had gone and they were never seen again.

One day, the sorcerer came to the door of a house in which lived three young women: Charlotte, Javotte and Finette, who made their living by spinning wool. Alone at home, the eldest, Charlotte, greeted the sorcerer with curiosity, for it was rare that they had visitors to their home. Seeing him in his ragged clothes, she immediately took pity on him.

'Please, miss,' he pleaded, 'I ask only for some bread.'

Charlotte hurried to the kitchen and returned with a loaf of bread. But as she reached out to hand it to him, the sorcerer snatched her up, locked her away in his basket and ran back into the forest.

The sorcerer returned to his house, where he freed Charlotte from the basket. She looked around in wonder, for everything he owned was quite magnificent: beautiful paintings adorned the walls, and furniture of the highest craftsmanship decorated each room. The house itself was enormous, and as he led her through its long corridors Charlotte thought she might never find her way out of it.

'You are to be the mistress of this house,' the sorcerer declared, 'and you will want for nothing, for everything you could possibly desire lies within these walls.'

But the sorcerer did not speak the truth, for he refused to grant Charlotte her greatest wish: to be reunited with Javotte and Finette. Instead, he imprisoned her against her will, and as the days passed she began to lose all hope of escape.

However, upon the rising of the next full moon, the sorcerer told Charlotte that he was leaving to go to town.

'Here are the keys to all the rooms in this house,' he said, handing her a set that hung from a brass hoop. 'You may go through any door you please, except the one that is opened by the smallest key.'

Charlotte stared at the key as she took it in her hands.

'Why?' she asked curiously. 'What lies beyond that door?'

The sorcerer's eyes narrowed.

'Misfortune and death,' he snarled, before leaving the grand house through its enormous oak door – and locking Charlotte inside.

As soon as the sorcerer was gone, Charlotte began to search for a way to escape. But all windows to the outside world were blocked with iron bars. Defeated, she instead decided to explore the house and, taking up the keys, one by one she entered every room. Some were filled with treasure: rubies, gold and silver that overflowed from heavy chests. In others she found dusty books, unusual creatures in jars and bunches of herbs that hung from the ceiling.

After many hours of searching, Charlotte finally found the door with a lock that fitted the smallest key – the forbidden room the sorcerer had told her not to enter. Although she was afraid of what she might find, Charlotte's curiosity got the better of her. Slowly, she turned the key in the lock and opened the door, stepping inside.

Charlotte gasped at the scene that appeared in front of her. The room was full of skeletons, which she supposed to be the missing girls from her town. The keys fell from Charlotte's shaking hands, and as she snatched them up, she saw that they were now stained with blood, which lay in puddles on the floor. Running to the bathroom, she tried to wash the keys, but no matter how much she scrubbed she could not remove the traces of blood upon them.

Suddenly Charlotte heard the front door of the house open and she shook with fear, for the sorcerer had returned.

'My love,' he hissed as he found Charlotte in the bathroom, 'where are my keys?'

Charlotte trembled and handed them to him. The sorcerer frowned. He saw at once from the red spatters upon them that Charlotte had disobeyed him and gone into the forbidden chamber.

'Since you have gone there against my will, you shall go back there against your own!' he cried, and dragged her away.

***

A few months later, the sorcerer returned to the town, dressed as a beggar with his basket on his back, and again sought out the house of the spinners.

Javotte was the kindest of the spinners, and the most generous of all. When she opened the door to the sorcerer, she felt deeply for his plight. She offered him *two* loaves of bread – but, just as he had done with Charlotte, the sorcerer seized Javotte and carried her off.

Poor Javotte fared no better than Charlotte, imprisoned against her will in the house in the dark heart of the forest. When the full moon rose and the sorcerer left her alone with the key to the forbidden room, she too entered it in the hope of finding an escape. And, just as Charlotte had before her, she dropped the keys in horror at what she saw there. Again the wicked sorcerer flew into a rage on learning of her disobedience, and soon Javotte had joined Charlotte in the bloody chamber.

***

As autumn turned to winter, the sorcerer grew restless and once again left the forest to prey on the unsuspecting young women of the town. He journeyed to the spinners' house, and this time his knock was answered by the brave and clever Finette. He tricked her into offering him some soup, and hurled her into his basket before hurrying away.

When the next full moon came, the sorcerer left Finette with the same instructions he had given the girls before her. Finette disobeyed him too, and after exploring the house soon found herself in the forbidden chamber. Discovering the skeletons of Charlotte and Javotte in that hellish room, Finette wept. But she was so brave that she did not shake nor drop the keys on the floor. Instead, deep within her, anger raged, and she swore to avenge them.

Gently, she took their bones and laid them on the ground, placing feet against ankles and elbows against arms. And as she tenderly placed their heads down against their necks, the bodies of the girls magically became whole again, just as they had been when they were alive. Charlotte and

Javotte opened their eyes and sat up, and in disbelief Finette drew them close. They kissed and caressed one another, and celebrated being born anew.

Together, the girls did the same with the other bones in the chamber, until a dozen women now stood amongst them. All of them were pleased to have been brought back to life, but their happiness was fleeting, for there was still no way to escape the sorcerer's home.

'My love, are you there?'

It was the sorcerer's voice. Realizing that he had returned, Finette told the girls to remain in the chamber, and hurried to meet him.

'Oh, how wonderful that you are back!' she lied.

'Did you go into the room I forbade you to enter?' the sorcerer asked.

Finette shook her head, and handed him the keys, upon which he saw not a single drop of blood.

'You have passed the test!' the sorcerer exclaimed. 'And as a reward I shall make you my bride.'

'What a happy occasion,' Finette replied, forcing a smile. 'But if we are to be married, please may we invite my family to the wedding? And perhaps send them some of the great treasures you have in your home, for they are very poor.'

The sorcerer grumbled. He did not believe in charity, even though he accepted it willingly in his disguise as a beggar. But so happy was he on this day that he agreed to Finette's request.

'Oh, wise husband-to-be,' Finette flattered him, 'you are so generous. I will fill your basket with these gracious gifts, so you can get going. On your way, be sure to invite all your friends. And whilst you are gone, I will prepare for the wedding. Go in haste! The sooner you're back, the sooner I'll be your wife!'

While the sorcerer put his boots back on, Finette set in motion a cunning plan. Instead of gold and jewels, in the sorcerer's basket she hid Charlotte and Javotte. Then she dragged it to the front door, where the sorcerer heaved it on to his back and, panting for breath, set off for the town in such a hurry he forgot to lock the front door. When she saw that he was safely away, Finette released the forbidden chamber's remaining prisoners, who ran from the house of horrors into the forest beyond.

Along the path through the woods, the sorcerer called at the homes of his friends – who, like him, were all wicked people – and invited them to his house for the wedding. Eventually, he arrived at the house of the spinners, where he left the basket and an invitation at the door, before hurrying back towards his home.

Meanwhile, Finette laid out a lavish feast for the wedding, though she had no intention of being any part of the celebrations. When she had finished, she took a sack filled with grain and drew upon it a face. She placed it in one of the upstairs windows, staring out at the world beyond. Upon it she placed a wreath of flowers, like a bridal crown.

Next, she returned to the kitchens, took off her dress and climbed into a barrel of honey. Clambering out again, she headed upstairs and tore open a mattress on one of the beds. A thousand feathers poured out on to the floor, in which Finette rolled until she looked not like herself but like a magnificent bird. She hurried to the front door, slipped the key into her feathers and fled the house, her steps so light with the joy of freedom that she soared through the forest like an eagle taking to the air.

Along the way she passed the sorcerer's wicked friends coming to the wedding. And, not long after, she came face to face with the sorcerer himself.

Finette soared through the forest like an eagle taking to the air.

'Who are you?' he asked her.

'I am a bird,' Finette replied. 'I have just passed your home, and seen many people arriving there for your wedding.'

'And what is the bride doing?' asked the sorcerer excitedly.

'She has swept the house from cellar to garret,' said Finette. 'And now she's looking out from the windows, excited for your return.'

The sorcerer looked up at the house and, just as the bird had said, he saw a face looking out at him from the window, wearing a bridal crown of flowers. The sorcerer grinned, and carried on his way, as Finette continued on hers until she reached the town and her home. There she was relieved to find Charlotte and Javotte, and the other freed women, who had gathered the citizens together and revealed the gruesome truth behind the mystery of their disappearance.

Led by the three spinners, the women took up

their arms and marched to the house in the dark heart of the forest. And there, as the sorcerer and his friends gathered around the wedding feast, waiting for the bride to come downstairs, Finette took the key from her feathers and locked the front door so that none of the evil within might escape.

And then they burned the house to the ground.

Marco and the Mountain of Gold

Illustrated by

Ez Silva

Only a handful of explorers had ever dared to make the dangerous voyage to the mysterious Mountain of Gold. From its roots deep in the Atlantic Ocean, its tip rose above the surface, forming an island from which few had ever returned. Some fishermen claimed they had seen it from their boats, fringed with sandy beaches of gold dust. Others said that on a clear day it could be seen upon the distant horizon, a glistening peak reflecting the rays of the sun.

But, despite its beauty, the island was said to be a lifeless, lonely place where not even a fly would go, for no creature can feed on gold, whatever its worth. Over time, the island became the stuff of legend, known amongst the islanders of the region as the place no one could go.

Mouro Grande, on the other hand, was an island full of life. Many ships stopped there on their voyages around the world, making it a place where a dozen cultures collided, filling its markets with food and textiles from three continents. Beyond the market was the palace, home to the king and queen and their son and heir, the spoilt Prince Bonito.

Upon the eve of his eighteenth birthday, Bonito could not sleep, plagued by a disturbing dream. In his mind's eye, he saw a princess of his own age who called him by his name and told him her own: Aldraga Jiliana. On waking, the prince refused the breakfast that his page brought him. Worried, the queen took her son to his father, and they asked him what was wrong.

'I dreamt of the most beautiful girl in the world,' said the prince, 'but she lives on the Mountain of Gold, the place no one may go. Many great heroes have attempted to climb its peak, but all have failed. I want to be with her very much, but, alas, I cannot.'

As Bonito returned to his bed, the king and the queen feared his spirit would not recover unless they could find the girl of his dreams. And so the king called upon his subjects for a volunteer with the courage to journey to the Mountain of Gold. He offered a chest filled with rubies, and a royal title too, to the warrior who could bring him Aldraga Jiliana. However, everyone in Mouro Grande had heard stories of the foolish men who had perished on the

Mountain of Gold, and not even the king's reward was enough to tempt them to risk their lives on Bonito's behalf.

But amongst the king's servants was a very brave and clever stable boy, whose name was Marco. He was the same age as the prince, but had grown up poor. His bed was the straw of the stables where he tended the horses, donkeys and mules, and his food was the scraps that the cook threw out for the animals to eat. Determined to win the king's prize and change his life, Marco lit a candle and gently placed his rosary upon a picture of San Pedro, gifted to him by his mother before her passing. He pressed his hands together, closed his eyes, and said:

'Dear godfather, can you hear me?
San Pedro, are you there?
Tell me the way to the Mountain of Gold,
I hope you hear my prayer.'

Slowly, Marco opened his eyes. But all he saw was the darkness of the stable. He sighed, and turned to the candle to blow it out when, much to his surprise, a voice began to speak from its flame.

'Dear godson, listen carefully, and I will tell you what to do . . .'

***

The next day, Marco stood before the king and bowed, offering to make the journey to retrieve the princess. But the king and his court laughed at him.

'And how do you think you will find the Mountain of Gold, when no one knows where it is?' the king said.

'I asked my godfather, San Pedro,' Marco replied, 'and he told me the way.'

The courtiers roared with laughter again, and Marco blushed.

'As if our gracious saint would take you as his godson,' said the queen.

'Or have the time to talk to a stable boy who sleeps in the dirt!' added the king. But he saw in Marco's eyes his determination to prove them wrong.

'Very well,' the king scoffed. 'Take whatever you need, and if you *should* find the princess, I'll make you a prince too!'

Marco nodded, and as the courtiers jeered him he left the palace. He gathered together the provisions that his godfather had told him to take – a sack of salt and a beautiful blue handkerchief – and went upon his way.

When he reached the coast, Marco walked to the water's edge. There, he did as San Pedro had ordered, and emptied the salt into the sea.

'Open up!' Marco cried.

To his amazement, the waves parted, revealing a long road. Marco followed the road for three days and nights, during which he saw no living things, not even a single bird. Exhausted, he finally arrived at the foot of the Mountain of Gold. Looking up, he felt discouraged, for the mountain seemed impossibly high. But Marco wanted desperately to prove wrong those who had doubted him, and so he gripped the golden rocks and began to climb.

It took a whole day, but at long last he pulled himself on to the summit. There he found a little house, and knocked upon its door. A maid answered and stared at him curiously.

'Who are you?' she asked. 'And what do you want?'

'I am Marco, and I have come to see Princess Aldraga Jiliana,' the stable boy explained.

'The princess is forbidden by her parents to leave this house,' said the maid. 'Tell me your message and I will deliver it to her for you.'

Marco scratched his forehead, thinking.

'I am very thirsty – could I please have something to drink first?'

The maid rolled her eyes.

'Wait here,' she said, closing the door in his face.

A moment later, the maid returned and gave Marco a cup of water. After he had drunk it, he took the handkerchief from his pocket and wiped his mouth. On seeing it, the maid gasped, and hurried back inside.

'Princess,' she exclaimed. 'That man at the door has the most beautiful handkerchief, the colour of the sea!'

'Then ask him to sell it to me,' the princess replied, 'for I would like to see it too.'

The maid returned to Marco and made the princess's offer. Marco laughed.

'A handkerchief is nothing – I am happy to give it to her,' he said, beaming. 'Her Highness needn't pay for such a small thing.'

The maid smiled, and reached out to take the handkerchief from him. But Marco did not let go of it.

'The only thing is that she must take it from me herself,' he continued. 'If she cannot leave this house, tell her to reach out for it through the window.'

The maid went back inside, and soon enough the princess reached her arm out of the window, her palm open. Marco took her hand in his and looked into her eyes.

'Princess, if you wish to leave, then say the word and you are free.'

The princess nodded enthusiastically, for she had long wished to escape the island but no one had ever been able to get to her before. Marco helped her climb out of the window and on to his back, and he climbed down to the foot of the mountain as fast as he could. Then Marco and Aldraga fled back along the road through the

Marco took her hand in his and looked into her eyes.
'Princess, if you wish to leave, then say the word and you are free.'

waves to the island of Mouro Grande and the palace.

The king and queen and their courtiers were shocked to see Marco again, and even more surprised that he had returned with the princess, just as he had promised. They took Aldraga to Prince Bonito's chambers, and on seeing her he was immediately cured of his melancholy.

'The girl of my dreams!' he cried, rising to his feet to embrace her. 'Will you marry me?'

Marco stood with the courtiers in the doorway. Everybody stared at the princess, waiting for her reaction. But Princess Aldraga did not speak. Instead, she groaned.

The king, the queen and their son looked at her, confused.

'What does she mean?' the king asked. 'Why does the princess refuse to speak? What kind of misfit have you brought me, stable boy? Forget your reward, and return to your straw bed.'

Heartbroken, Marco did as the king ordered and left the palace. The king had betrayed him and he had gone on his journey for nothing. There were no rubies in his pockets, and no royal title to his name.

In the weeks that followed, Prince Bonito attempted to get an answer from the princess, but she refused to say a single word. In frustration, his father eventually declared: 'Whoever can make the princess speak shall take her as his wife!'

Many men came to the palace and knelt before the princess, asking her if she would take them as her husband, but to each she groaned and said no word – until one day Marco appeared.

Marco had consulted with San Pedro, and again he had offered his advice. The stable boy returned to the palace with a violin, and asked for the king's permission to see the princess. The court gathered and nervously watched as Marco approached Aldraga. As he tuned the violin, Aldraga's eyes flicked in his direction, and as he began to play, her lips unlocked, and she began to sing.

When Aldraga's song ended, the courtiers clapped their hands, delighted to finally hear her beautiful voice. But the king and the queen did not share their enthusiasm. They watched, humiliated, as Aldraga and Marco talked and laughed together for the rest of the evening, and it was apparent to the whole court that a common stable boy had won the princess's love, and not the king and queen's son.

Because his courtiers all adored Princess Aldraga, who was kind and gracious to everyone she met, the king knew he had to keep his promise that Marco could marry her. But as preparations for the wedding began, the queen started to search for secrets in Marco's past that she might use to disrupt the forthcoming marriage.

The eve of the wedding came, and hundreds of islanders gathered to celebrate the union. During the festivities one of the queen's handmaids arrived with some information. In the year of Marco's birth, the king had issued a census to be carried out throughout the island, and upon it Marco's mother had recorded his name as Marta, declaring him her daughter.

The queen hurried to the king and Prince Bonito to show them the census, but both her husband and her son were unconvinced.

'Marco is a man,' said Bonito with a shrug.

'Of course he is,' his father agreed. 'It is plain for all to see.'

Angrily, the queen grabbed their hands and marched them towards Marco and Aldraga's chamber, intent on proving them wrong. The queen determined to tell Aldraga what she had learned, in the hope the princess would cast Marco aside and marry Prince Bonito instead.

But as they spied at Marco's door, they heard that he had already begun to tell the princess his story.

'Aldraga, before we wed, I need to tell you something,' said Marco.

'What is it?' asked the princess.

'Once they called me Marta, but it is Marco who I have truly always been.'

The princess laid her hand upon his shoulder and squeezed it gently. She wrapped her arms round him and held him close.

'I grew up in a kingdom where there are only women, who live and love together,' she whispered. 'If I have learned one thing from my journey, it is that all should live and love as they so wish. I chose not Prince Bonito . . . I choose you.'

The king, the queen and Bonito burst into the room, where they discovered Marco and Aldraga in their embrace. Just as they did so, a candle in the window burst into flame, and from its light came a voice.

'I am Marco's godfather, San Pedro,' the light said. 'Marco is a man and the prince this kingdom needs.'

The king, the queen and Bonito immediately fell to their knees, for they feared San Pedro more than they feared any other thing.

And so it was that the wedding ceremony went ahead, and Marco became a prince, as he was promised. And he and Princess Aldraga later became king and queen themselves, ruling the island with open minds and hearts.

THE TALE OF THE RABBIT GOD

Illustrated by

Jenn So

Hu Tianbao was just eighteen years old, but his palms bore the scars and bruises of many years' hard labour.

Each day, he rose early to serve the household in which he was employed as a gardener, tending to the flowers and fruits of a blossoming orchard. His master regularly sent him into the town on errands, which Hu dreaded, for along the way he had to pass the house of the rich merchant Mr Shan.

Mr Shan had a belly so round it was a wonder

his two little legs could carry him about. He had made a great fortune, and spent it on lavish furnishings and treasures to decorate his grand house. He had three sons – Dishi, Feng and Chao – who, like their father, were fat from feasting on the delicious meals their cook made for them each night. The boys were so spoilt they knew nothing of the hardships of others, and loved to taunt those less fortunate than themselves. Whenever Hu passed, the bullies would call him names as they lounged in the sunshine.

'Tuzi!' they shouted. 'Run away fast or we'll beat you with a stick!'

Hu hated the nickname the cruel boys had coined for him. It meant 'rabbit' – a common slur for men who loved men. But what worried him most of all was how they had uncovered his secret.

One day, whilst Hu was washing the gates of his master's house, the bullies passed by and saw him. They kicked over Hu's bucket, drenching him in soapy water, and erupted into menacing laughter as they drew closer. Hu raised his fists, ready to fight, knowing all too well that he was outnumbered.

However, just as the boys prepared to throw their first punches, the sound of galloping hooves turned their heads to the street. A mighty stallion approached, ridden by the most handsome man Hu had ever seen.

Dingbang was something of a prodigy. At a very early age he had been selected to become the governor of Fujian province. Not only was he extremely intelligent, but Dingbang was also fiercely loyal and believed above all else in upholding the laws of the land. He dressed simply, his long, thick hair tied back in a neat bun that accentuated the strong lines of his face.

Halting his horse between Hu and the bullies, Dingbang raised his sword.

'Enough!' he shouted at the boys. 'Go to your homes and make mischief there instead!'

Terrified, the boys ran away, leaving Dingbang and Hu alone. Hu bowed gratefully.

'Thank you,' he said, 'for saving me from death.'

Dingbang nodded before galloping away.

In the weeks that followed, Hu could not stop thinking about his brief meeting with Dingbang. One day, whilst gathering firewood from the forest, Hu walked along the river. It was summer, and the heat had driven many of the villagers to the cool water to swim. As he approached, Hu gasped. Dingbang was amongst the bathers and Hu could not draw his eyes away.

Suddenly Hu felt something strike his back: a rock, thrown by the bully brothers, who were running towards him. They grabbed Hu and dragged him down to the riverbank.

'Everyone! Hu has been spying on you, watching you bathe!' they shouted, startling

Dingbang, who quickly returned to the bank and retrieved his clothes. Embarrassed, Hu looked up at the faces of the other men and women who were bathing in the river, but they looked back at him in disgust.

Once he was dressed, Dingbang approached the boys, who held Hu down on his knees.

'Is what they say true?' he asked. 'Were you looking at the bathers?'

Hu sighed, shaking his head.

'Not at the bathers, my lord, but at you. Ever since I first saw you, I haven't been able to forget you,' Hu admitted. 'Please forgive me.'

But Dingbang valued the laws of the land above all else.

'If you admit you are guilty of spying on the bathers, then for your crime you must pay the price,' he said, shaking his head, disappointed. Dingbang mounted his horse and, to Hu's horror, galloped away.

The sun was setting, and the other bathers gathered their clothes and fled the lake too, leaving Hu alone with the merchant's cruel sons, abandoned to the judgment of the world's worst jury.

The boys were quick to make their decision and dragged Hu into the river. There they held him underwater until his world became nothing but darkness . . .

But in death Hu followed a light that led him to a vast oasis. Here he met the spirits of the afterlife, who prepared to make a judgement of their own. Hu fell to his knees before them.

'I deserved to die,' Hu cried, 'for I fell in love with a nobleman and offended him. But I did love him very much, and it was not just a temporary infatuation. I never harmed him or anyone else.'

The spirits took pity on Hu, and none of them shared the disgust or anger of Dingbang and the bully boys. After conferring with one another, they decided to change the fate of the loyal gardener and granted him the gifts of a god. Reclaiming the word he was once called as a badge of shame, the spirits gave Hu a new name – Tu'er Shen, the Rabbit God – and made him the protector of men who love men.

A few weeks after Hu's death at the hands of Dishi, Feng and Chao, the boys' father was asleep in his enormous bed. But his snores were interrupted when he felt something jump upon his chest. Opening his eyes, he saw a rabbit staring back at him, its nose twitching.

Mr Shan shrieked so loudly that his scream carried through the house. His three sons sat up in their beds, shocked. They hurried to their father's chamber and burst into the room, worried that a thief had attacked their father in the night.

'Father, what is wrong?' they asked. But he turned to them, angry.

Reclaiming the word he was once called as a badge of shame, the spirits gave Hu a new name – Tu'er Shen, the Rabbit God, the protector of men who love men.

'Murderers!' he cried. 'A rabbit came to me this night and told me of your crimes. You shamed an innocent and led him to his death. The gods themselves have called upon me to right your wrongs, and you shall help me carry out their orders.'

In the weeks that followed, Mr Shan counted the fortune he had amassed over his lifetime. He took the money he had intended to become his sons' inheritance and instead used it to build a beautiful temple in the heart of the town. He employed his lazy sons as labourers, and made them sweat in the midday heat, carrying bricks and laying tiles, working from sunrise to sunset with no pay. Many of the townsfolk who had been victims of the cruel boys' pranks could not help but smile that they had finally got their comeuppance.

Eventually, the temple was finished – the Temple of the Rabbit God. All across China, people learned of Hu Tianbao's story, and came to the temple to make offerings of incense to Tu'er Shen. For every man since who has wished for a love affair with another man, the temple has been a place for them to pray and hope and dream.

The Soldier and the Peasant

Illustrated by

Nontira Kigle

Once upon a time in Germany, there was a farm owned by a very rich man. Each day he stood in the yard and looked out upon his prosperous land: the corn grew tall, the trees bore fruit, and the grain filled the barn in enormous heaps that stretched from the ground to the rafters. In the stable, the oxen, cows and horses rested, fat and content from their feeding. As the day turned to dusk, the rich man returned to his grand house, where he spent the evening counting his money (his favourite hobby) before returning each coin to a huge iron chest.

However, one night this routine was interrupted. Much to his surprise, the rich man heard a knock, but it was not at the door of his home. It was at the door of his heart. As it opened, he heard a voice inside his mind.

What good have you done with these coins you count? it asked. *Have you given help to the poor? Have you shared your bread with the hungry? Have you been content with what you possess, or did you always desire to have more?*

The rich man's heart was racing . . . and he felt it answer back.

I have been hard on others and lacked pity, his heart admitted. *I have never shown kindness to my own family. If a beggar came to ask for help, I turned them away. I have not troubled myself with God, but instead have thought only of increasing my wealth. Even if everything in the world belonged to me, I would still not have had enough.*

The rich man clutched his chest as he realized this truth. He sat down, fearing his trembling knees would cause him to fall.

Another knock, this time at the door of his house, caused his heart to race again. Fearful, the rich man walked into the hall and slowly opened the door. There stood a man – his neighbour, Lukas.

Lukas was a very poor man, the single parent of six children for whom he struggled to provide, despite labouring day and night. He had long contemplated asking his neighbour for help, but knew that the rich man would surely turn him away. However, tonight, as he watched his children share their last mouldy crust of bread, Lukas had decided that he had no other option.

He bowed his head, and humbly said, 'I know that you do not like to share, but I feel like I am drowning. My children are starving. Please, lend me a sack of corn.'

The rich man frowned, and stared at Lukas, crossing his arms in thought. For the first time in his life, his greed began to melt away, replaced with mercy and sympathy.

'I will not lend you a sack of corn,' he said eventually, and Lukas sighed with disappointment. But the rich man had not finished. 'I will *give* you two sacks instead as a gift – on one condition.'

'What would you like me to do?' Lukas asked, beyond grateful for the rich man's kindness.

The rich man raised his hand and pointed towards a churchyard in the distance.

'When I am dead,' he said, 'you must spend three nights at my graveside, watching over me.'

It was a rather disturbing request, but a deal that Lukas could not afford to turn down. He shook the rich man's hand, and returned home, the two sacks of corn slung over his shoulders.

Three days later, Lukas was shocked to learn that the rich man had died. Haunted by their final encounter, he thought back over their conversation; it was almost as if the rich man had known his death was close. As he laboured in the fields, Lukas asked the other workers what had happened, but none knew how the man had died. In fact, few were even interested, and no one grieved for the miserable old man who'd hoarded his wealth from those in need.

On the day of the rich man's funeral, Lukas was the only mourner. He was an honourable man, and remembered his promise as he watched his neighbour's coffin lowered into the earth. After all, for the last few days his children had eaten until they were full every night, thanks to the gift of corn.

As the priest and the gravediggers left the churchyard, Lukas remained, sitting upon the grave mound. He looked up to the moon, and listened to the sad, soft hoots of an owl, the only sound to break the silence. There he stayed all night long, until the sun finally rose, and he hurried to work.

He returned the second night, which passed as quietly as the first. However, on the third and final night, as he sat upon the grave, Lukas began to feel a creeping fear, as if something strange might happen at any moment. Shivering in the cold night air, he was startled by the crack of a twig, and looked up to see a man approaching whom he'd never seen before.

The man, like himself, was middle-aged, and he had a scar upon his cheek. His riding boots clomped on the dry mud path. He wore a long, brown and tattered cloak, its seams frayed. Upon seeing Lukas, his hazel eyes narrowed in suspicion.

'What are you looking for here?' asked Lukas nervously. 'Aren't you afraid to be in a graveyard so late at night?'

The man considered Lukas, and then the rich man's grave.

'I'm not looking for anything,' he replied, 'and I'm afraid of nothing. I was a soldier, until I was wounded in battle. Now I have nothing but the clothes on my back, and no home to call my own. I'm looking for a place to sleep, and here be as good as any. My name is Wolf.'

Lukas thought for a moment. The rich man hadn't said he had to watch over his grave alone. The churchyard was an eerie place and he welcomed Wolf's company.

'If you fear nothing,' said Lukas, 'then stay with me a while to watch over this grave, because I'm worried something bad is going to happen.'

'Keeping watch was my job as a soldier,' said Wolf with a smile, 'so I'd be glad to help. Whatever we face tonight, be it good or evil, we'll confront it together.'

Lukas beckoned Wolf to join him at his side,

sitting atop the grave mound. They shared some bread that Lukas had brought with him, and a flask of water, and talked for many hours.

Wolf had lived an adventurous life, and Lukas was comforted listening to him recount his stories. Sharing his own, he told Wolf about his children, and how he had raised them alone. He opened up about his struggles, and how, at his lowest point, he had begged the rich man for help. Wolf took the peasant's hand in his and, without any more words, they sat in silence for a while, grateful to have met another who understood their pain.

Suddenly they heard a shrill whistle, and turned to see a figure standing before them. Terrified, they recognized him as the devil himself. The devil grinned, and raised his finger, his nail long like a claw.

'Leave this place,' the devil hissed, pointing at the grave mound upon which they sat. 'The buried

Wolf and Lukas turned to see a figure standing before them. Terrified, they recognized him as the devil himself.

man belongs to me, and I'm here to take him away. Step aside, or I'll wring your necks and take you as well.'

The brave soldier refused to move. He put his arm round Lukas protectively, and said, 'You are not my captain, and I will neither obey nor fear you. We are sitting here until the sun rises, and it's you who needs to leave.'

The devil raised his eyebrows. It had been some time since anyone had defied him, and he was both annoyed and impressed. He stared at the soldier and the peasant, and laughed. He could see from their worn clothes that they were as poor as vagabonds, and that money would prove to be their greatest temptation.

The devil smiled, reaching into his coat and removing a purse, which he placed gently on the ground before them.

'Take this purse of gold coins home with you,' he said softly.

Wolf and Lukas looked at each other, then at the devil again, and shook their heads.

'It's a worthy offer,' said Wolf, 'but a small purse of gold is not enough for both of us. If you want us to leave, fill one of my boots with gold instead.'

'I don't carry that amount around with me,' said the devil, irritated. 'So I suppose I will have to fetch it.'

With that, he vanished, much to Lukas and Wolf's relief. Lukas looked into Wolf's eyes, searching for reassurance, but he could see that Wolf was as nervous as he was.

The soldier stood, removed his boot and placed it on the grave. He took the knife that the peasant had brought to cut the bread, and sliced into its sole, removing it completely. He then searched the long grass that grew around the rich man's grave, until he found a hole in the earth into which he reached his arm.

'OK, this is deep enough. Pass me the boot, my friend.'

Lukas passed Wolf the boot, which he placed over the hole, carefully covering it with overgrown weeds until it disappeared from view. Just as Wolf returned to his seat beside Lukas on the grave, the devil reappeared, this time with a purse in each hand.

'That won't be enough,' said Wolf, shaking his head, 'but put them into my boot and we'll see.'

The devil knelt beside the grave, and poured the coins from each purse into the boot. Just as Wolf had predicted, the boot was clearly far from being full.

'See?' said the soldier. 'Until it's full, we refuse to leave.'

The devil cursed and clicked his fingers, vanishing again.

On his return he carried a bag of coins so heavy that his back bent under its weight. He untied it, and poured the contents into the boot, smiling cruelly as he listened to the gold coins clinking as they tumbled upon one another. When the bag was empty, the devil peered into the boot – but all he could see was darkness.

'It's still not enough to strike a bargain,' said Wolf, shrugging with a wry smile.

The devil glared at him, his eyes burning red with anger. Once more he snapped his fingers and spirited away, returning with a sack so large he had to carry it over his shoulders. He poured hundreds of coins into the boot, and waited for it to finally overflow with riches. But, just as before, the boot failed to become full.

Enraged, the devil reached out towards the soldier and the peasant, as if to grab their necks, but as he did, the first rays of the sun broke through the dawn clouds, falling on his face. The devil screamed and fled, and Wolf and Lukas hugged each other. They had saved the rich man's soul.

'Should we divide it between us?' asked Lukas as Wolf scooped the gold coins out of the hole. But Wolf shook his head.

'Give my share to those who need it more than me,' he said, pulling on his broken boot and looking towards the path, as if wondering where he might travel next. But Lukas did not want him to leave quite so soon.

'Then come to live with me,' he offered, 'and share my portion of the gold.'

And so Wolf did just that. They returned to Lukas's cottage, where they spent the rest of their long and peaceful lives together, and the children they raised never went hungry again.

THE IVORY CITY

Illustrated by

Anshika Khullar

Our story begins in India, where a member of the royal household had found himself accused of a terrible crime.

Prince Kavin was the most handsome young man in the kingdom, and of late his father had met with many other great leaders who wished for their daughters to marry him. But the young prince was not interested in any of the girls, preferring instead the company of his best friend Darshan, son of the king's chief vizier.

Through the friendship of their fathers, the boys

had known each other all their lives. Now approaching eighteen years of age, they spent every day together. The king approved of their friendship and believed that the vizier's obedient son had been a good influence on his heir. When the prince was headstrong, Darshan was cautious. If the prince was foolish, Darshan was resourceful. If the prince felt fearful, Darshan would appear at his side to offer him his courage. And, on this day in particular, the prince needed Darshan's reassuring guidance more than ever . . .

The prince rose, as he often did, in the mood for fun. He leapt from his bed and reached for his bow and arrows, which hung from a nail on the wall. Hurrying to Darshan's room, he jumped on the bed, waking his sleeping friend.

'Get up!' said the prince. 'It's a beautiful day, and we have mischief to make!'

'It's four in the morning,' groaned Darshan. But he knew that to argue with the prince was fruitless, and he obediently pulled on his clothes and followed the prince out into the gardens as the sun rose over the palace.

The prince loved to practise archery, but Darshan found that the activity tested his nerves, for the prince was careless with his aim, and tended to fire his arrows in all directions.

'Relax, Darshan!' Kavin laughed as his friend cowered behind a tree for safety. 'There is no one about. Stop hiding like a mouse.'

But Darshan was right to be cautious, for no sooner had the prince declared there was nothing to fear than one of his careless arrows went flying over the palace walls. Dropping from the sky, it fell through a window into a neighbouring house and grazed the arm of a merchant's wife as she ate breakfast, peacefully looking out at the rising sun. Horrified, she fainted, her body falling to the floor with a great thud, awaking her husband.

When the woman recovered, the merchant stormed into the palace and stood before the king.

'Your reckless son shot my beloved wife!' he exclaimed. 'Something must be done!'

Humiliated, the king summoned Kavin before him.

'What kind of example are you setting for our people?' the king asked his son. 'By law, you should be executed for a crime as serious as this.'

The vizier quickly stepped in to soothe his king's growing anger.

'Your Majesty,' he said, 'let us investigate the facts. Boys, why have you done this terrible thing?'

The prince was ashamed and stared at the ground.

'I shot an arrow at a bird,' he explained, 'but I missed, and the arrow flew over the wall and struck the merchant's wife. Had I known she was near, I would not have fired in that direction.'

The king tapped his fingers repeatedly upon the arms of his throne, deep in thought. Everyone present knew better than to speak. Eventually, the king reached a decision.

'The laws of this country have been made for all, and you are not above them,' he said to his son sternly. 'Until you have learned that, you are banished from this land.'

Kavin nodded as tears streamed down his face. He had escaped the penalty of death, but would now have to leave behind everything and everyone he loved. Satisfied, the merchant and his wife left. However, as Kavin turned to his father to bid him farewell, the king could not hide his disappointment in his son, dismissing him with a wave of his hand.

The next morning, seven soldiers accompanied the prince out of the city gates. Here, Kavin was surprised to find Darshan waiting for him with two horses and all the supplies he had been able to gather in such a short space of time.

'I'm coming with you,' said Darshan, throwing his arms round the prince's neck, 'because I can't let you go alone. We have lived together, we will be exiled together, and we will die together.'

Kavin was moved by Darshan's promise, but worried that it was his friend, for once, who was acting on impulse.

'Think about what you are doing,' he answered. 'All kinds of trials lie before me. Why should you leave your home, your father and your country, and risk your life to be with me on this journey?'

Defiant, Darshan took the prince's hand in his.

'Because I love you,' Darshan replied, 'and I'd never be happy without you. If you love me, don't turn me away.'

And so, as day turned to dusk, the guards accompanied Prince Kavin and Darshan until they reached the border. From there they continued into the unknown world beyond, walking hand in hand, their horses carrying their few remaining possessions behind them. That night, they huddled together, the prince's arm wrapped round Darshan's waist under the blanket they shared for warmth.

'Thank you for coming with me,' Kavin whispered as they stared at the stars overhead.

***

Some days later, the young exiles came to a large tree near a stream, with a village beyond. As Prince Kavin gathered sticks to make a fire, Darshan went into the village to buy provisions for their dinner.

After some time waiting for Darshan to return, the prince grew impatient and decided to go for a walk. Following the stream, he soon discovered a beautiful lake. Magnificent lotus flowers drifted across the calm waters, and water plants curled over its green banks. Thirsty, the prince knelt at the lake's edge and scooped some water into his palms. But as he drew them to his lips to drink, he noticed something in the water – the image of a girl's glistening face.

Astonished, Kavin dropped the water, but on turning round he could find no one behind him. Thinking that he must be seeing things, he took more water in his hands – and once again saw the reflection in his palm. This time as he looked up he saw, sitting upon the bank of the lake, a fairy princess.

The wings of the fairy princess caught the light of the sun as if each fibre had been sewn in silk. She stared back at Kavin with dark brown eyes, and looked him up and down curiously. Then she smiled – and the prince immediately fell helplessly in love with her.

Back at their camp, Darshan returned from the village to discover the fire alight, but Kavin was nowhere to be seen. Following Kavin's footprints, Darshan tracked him to the lake where he found the prince lying unconscious by the water's edge.

'Alas! Alas!' cried Darshan, pouring water on to the prince's face to revive him. 'Please don't die! I couldn't bear it!'

Kavin opened his eyes and looked around, startled.

'What happened?' Darshan asked as he helped him to his feet.

The prince pushed him away, annoyed.

'Go away!' he snapped, to Darshan's surprise. 'Leave me alone. I don't even want to set eyes on you.'

Darshan stared back at Kavin, confused. 'But I've brought us food. Why don't we eat and then continue on our way?'

'Go alone,' the prince replied, his eyes as cold as stone.

Darshan had never seen his friend this way before, and his words hurt him deeply.

'What has happened to make you detest the sight of me so suddenly?' he asked.

The prince pointed to the bank of the lake.

'I saw a fairy,' he answered, 'but only for a moment. When she noticed I was staring at her, she covered her face with lotus petals. But even in that second I saw her beauty. Then she took out an ivory box and held it up towards me and I fainted. And now . . . I can't stop thinking about her.'

Darshan stared at where the prince had pointed. When Darshan was a child, his father the vizier had told him stories about the fairy folk that dwelled beyond their kingdom, and how he ought not to look upon them in case he should be enchanted. But if the prince had heard these tales too, he had obviously ignored the warnings. Darshan looked back at his friend, who was still staring at the lake, entranced. For a while, they stood in silence, until the prince finally spoke.

'If you can help me find her again,' Kavin said softly, 'I will go anywhere with you.'

The prince looked up at Darshan with such longing in his eyes that the vizier's son had never seen before in their many years of friendship. And to make the prince happy was all he wanted in the world.

'You have met Gulizar, the fairy princess of the Ivory City,' Darshan informed him.

'How do you know this?' Kavin asked, excited.

'From the signs she gave you,' Darshan replied. 'She covered her face with lotus petals to hide the rosy cheeks from which she earned her name. And because of the box she carried I know where she lives, for the Ivory City is where such things are made.'

'Then we must go there at once! Do you know the way?'

To make the prince happy was all Darshan wanted in the world.

Darshan forced a smile. 'I will help you to find her, and to her heart be wed.'

It broke his own heart to make this promise, but Darshan knew there was no antidote to such a spell. His friend was bound to love the fairy princess until his dying day. And should he not find her, he would likely lose his mind.

The prince felt reassured by Darshan's words, and so they ate, and then, at the prince's urging, continued on their journey. But not long after, just as night set in, they met a pair of men on the road.

'It's late,' said the men politely, 'and there is not another village for miles. Stay with us in our home until the morning.'

The prince was keen to accept their invitation, even though Darshan encouraged him to decline it.

'These men are clearly not to be trusted!' Darshan warned, but the prince rolled his eyes.

'You're always so serious,' he said, following

the men into the forest, Darshan reluctantly following behind.

But Darshan was right to be cautious. The men were from one of the most notorious families of robbers in the area, and lived in a tower upon a hill. Their practice was to trick those unfortunate enough to meet them into staying with them, offering shelter and kindness. But beneath the tower was a deep pit, into which they threw the bodies of such unlucky travellers, having first stolen everything from them.

And so it was only an hour later that the boys found themselves locked in a room into which they had been led with the promise of a meal and a warm fire. The prince groaned, his head in his arms, as Darshan sighed.

'There's no point moaning about it,' he said, by now quite used to the prince leading him into such situations. Darshan loved Kavin's trusting nature, but had to wonder when his friend would realize that being a prince made him a target for those who wished to benefit from his riches.

Instead of panicking, Darshan tried to think of a way for them to escape. Climbing to the window, he looked down at the ground, too far below to jump without being hurt. But a nearby wall seemed just within reach – if he had the courage to make the leap.

'Wait here – I'll be back soon,' Darshan told the prince. Then, taking a deep breath, he leapt across to the wall and climbed down to the foot of the tower.

Sneaking through the courtyard as the thieves slept, he discovered the housekeeper, a wrinkled woman at least a hundred years old, washing laundry. Darshan smiled, a new plan forming in his head.

Soon, with the help of the housekeeper, Darshan had obtained the keys to the prince's cell and freed him.

'How did you convince her to help us?' asked Kavin in amazement as the housekeeper handed them back their stolen belongings.

'I told her you'd marry her,' joked Darshan, much to the prince's horror.

The housekeeper led the boys to where their horses had been stabled. Now, though, they faced a new problem with their escape. Opening the gates of the tower would make such a noise it would wake the thieves. But the only other way out was by the smallest side door, through which a horse would never fit.

Darshan sat down, thinking back to his childhood when his father the vizier had told him stories about charms used by the ancients of the kingdom. Nervously, he stood and held his hand towards the horses. Quietly at first, then louder as he grew more confident, he spoke a magical spell.

Kavin and the housekeeper watched in astonishment as the horses shrank in size to no bigger than a mouse. Carefully picking them up, Darshan led the prince and the housekeeper through the little door to their freedom. Placing the horses back on the ground, Darshan returned them to their normal size and the boys quickly climbed upon their backs. The housekeeper sat behind the prince, gripping his waist tightly as they began to gallop away.

But they were not safe yet. Awaking to the sound of the horses' hooves, the thieves shot arrows at them from the tower. One struck the housekeeper, and she fell to the ground, dead. Forced to leave her behind, the boys rode on until the tower was just a tiny speck on the horizon – a distant memory and nightmare far behind them.

***

The pair rode on as days turned to weeks, asking each passer-by for directions to the Ivory City.

Eventually, as they crossed the peaks of three blue mountains, they arrived at their final destination – a huge city on the shores of a vast ocean.

The walls were so tall that little could be seen of the city they protected, apart from the distant scarlet steeple of a palace. The gates were closed, and the sun had already begun to set, so Kavin and Darshan decided to seek shelter in a small cottage just outside the walls.

They knocked on the door and an elderly woman answered. Darshan explained that they wished her no harm, and asked her for a bed for the night. Initially mistrusting the strangers, the old woman refused them, until Darshan offered to pay her for lodgings, water and a meal.

Having travelled such a long way, Kavin wanted to be sure that they had come to the right place.

'Has this city a name?' he asked the old woman, his mouth full as he wolfed down the food she had prepared for them. The old woman raised her eyebrows.

'Of course it has, you silly boy,' she said. 'Even villages have names, let alone a city so grand as this.'

'What is it, then?' asked Darshan.

'The Ivory City,' said the old woman. 'I thought its name was known all over the world.'

The prince sighed with relief.

'And does this city have a king?' Darshan enquired.

'Of course,' the woman replied. 'And a queen too. And the princess, Gulizar.'

Kavin sat up at the mention of the princess's name and sighed deeply again. The old woman shot him a curious glance as she left to prepare their room.

'See?' said Darshan. 'We have found your princess.' He could see that the prince was glad.

The next morning, the boys came down for

breakfast to find the old woman dressed in her best clothes, her hair arranged in a beautiful fashion.

'Are you expecting company?' asked Darshan, curious.

'No,' the old woman explained. 'I'm going to visit my daughter, who is one of Princess Gulizar's servants. I visit her every day. Apart from yesterday, because you two arrived to take up my time instead.'

But Darshan had watched the woman that morning, and seen how she gossiped with her neighbours, sharing secrets she'd been told in trust and discussing the private affairs of the other villagers. Darshan did not trust her, so he decided to put an idea into her head.

'Please don't mention us to the princess,' he pleaded. 'We have travelled from a far-off kingdom and would rather no one in the palace knew we are here.'

Darshan's plan worked. After breakfast, the

old woman left for the palace and no sooner had she arrived there than she began gossiping with Princess Gulizar about the strangers who had come to her home.

'One of them appears to be very stupid,' the old woman complained. 'He did not even know the name of the Ivory City, and they both seemed particularly interested in you, Your Highness. Where could they have come from that they didn't know of our city and yourself? I tell you, I'd throw them out were they not paying me so well for their stay – they are quite obviously very rich. I earned it, mind you. All I do is cook, and clean, and wash, and wait on them. I really don't understand how two boys can cause such a mess.'

Gulizar found the old woman annoying because she talked so much, and soon ordered her away. But she was a little curious about the strangers the old woman had mentioned.

Returning to her home, the old woman

admitted to Darshan she had not kept her promise but had told the princess everything. Darshan was pleased.

'Now the princess knows that a traveller from a far-off land has come to see her,' he explained to Kavin. 'She will wonder who you are. Soon you will be reunited.'

The next day, the old woman returned to the palace. Gulizar wasn't in the mood to hear more of the old woman's gossip, so as she approached Gulizar ordered one of her servants to be ready to come in with an excuse for Gulizar to leave if the woman should talk too long.

As expected, the old woman did exactly that, so after ten minutes the servant ran in with the most outrageous lie.

'Your Highness!' they cried. 'The king's elephants have escaped! They are rushing about the countryside causing all manner of chaos! I fear they've lost their minds!'

Worried that her cottage might get trampled, the old woman bade the princess a hasty farewell.

'I must return to my guests to ensure their safety,' she explained, though she was actually more concerned that the money her lodgers owed her might be destroyed.

'Let me help you on your journey,' offered the princess, nodding to her servant, who hurried out of her chamber for a moment, before returning with a swing.

The swing – a gift the princess had received from her parents on her eighteenth birthday – was enchanted with quite remarkable magic. Whoever sat on it would be whisked high into the air and dropped at whatever place they wished to go.

A little anxiously, the old woman sat upon it, closed her eyes and wished to return home. At once, she was swung into the sky, screaming, and flown at speed all the way back to the cottage, where the swing deposited her directly in her living room at the feet of Kavin and Darshan, who were rather surprised to see her.

The old woman's flight had left her shaking, one earring lost, her hair tangled all around her head. Fetching her a cup of water, Darshan asked her to tell them what had happened. The old woman explained, and Darshan soon reassured her that the princess had clearly played a trick on her, as no elephants had been seen in the area. Still shaken by her flight, the old woman retired to bed.

As soon as she was out of earshot, Darshan turned to Kavin, pointing at the magic swing.

'Prepare to meet your princess,' he said, 'for now we have the means to reach her.'

The prince and Darshan sat upon the swing, closed their eyes and wished to be carried to the princess. Once more, the swing flew through the skies, carrying its new passengers into the palace. Falling to the ground, the prince looked up to see the object of his search before him: the fairy princess Gulizar herself, who ran straight into his arms.

'Is it really you?' the princess asked, staring into Kavin's eyes. 'Please, let this not be a mirage because I want it so desperately to be true.'

'It is me. A thousand thanks to heaven for bringing me to you,' said the prince, embracing her.

As Kavin and Gulizar embraced, Darshan looked away, and took a deep breath. As happy as he was that the prince was no longer at risk of losing his mind, being forced to give him up to another felt a little like losing his own.

Darshan turned back to see the prince kneeling on the floor as the excited fairy princess accepted his proposal of marriage.

'Come on,' said Darshan eventually, pulling the young lovers apart. 'You have your whole lives to live together, but until your marriage you must part every night.'

With that, Darshan led the prince back to the old woman's cottage. From the spire of the palace, the princess watched them go, suspicious and ever so slightly jealous.

Who was this boy at her beloved's side who had taken him away from her?

***

The fairy princess Gulizar was extremely protective of the boy she loved. Though Prince Kavin came to visit her every day, the princess constantly worried about him when they were apart. She feared he might be captured by thieves again, or struck down by sickness, and that she'd lose him forever. So every night, as the prince prepared to leave the palace, the princess pleaded with him to stay with her.

'Why do you have to go?' she whined. 'Your friend Darshan is quite capable of looking after himself. Stay here with me instead.'

However, even enchantments can only reach so far into the heart, and there had been a time when Kavin's had been full with his love for life, his kingdom and Darshan. And, although it now pined for the princess and very little else, some feelings remained that her magic had not extinguished.

'I can't do that,' the prince explained. 'Darshan left everything for me – his home, his country and his father too. And if it had not been for his help I would never have met you. The least I can do is share an evening meal with him and keep him company in this city so far from home.'

'Is he also to share his evening meals with us when we are wed?' muttered Gulizar to herself.

As Kavin returned to his friend, Gulizar threw a glass across the room in exasperation, and swore very loudly. Though at first she had accepted Darshan's presence for the sake of pleasing her prince, she now decided she would like to be rid of him.

* * *

A few days later, Princess Gulizar prepared a delicious pulao dish with a secret ingredient – poison. As soon as the dish was cooked through, the princess placed a lid on the saucepan so that the poisonous steam might not escape. A servant then took the pot all the way from the palace to the old woman's cottage, where they delivered it to Darshan. A handwritten note from the princess was attached to the pot with a pink ribbon.

The Princess Gulizar sends you an offering in the name of friendship.

Darshan was surprised. On the few occasions he had met with the princess, she had been particularly frosty towards him, so he appreciated the gesture of friendship.

'Please send the princess my salaam,' he told her servant, bowing graciously.

As the servant returned to the palace, Darshan left the cottage and sat by the sea. He lifted the lid from the pot, and placed it down on the grass beside him. Just as he was about to tuck into the delicious dish, he remembered that he should first wash his hands, and ran down to the sea to do so. But on returning to the pot, he noticed that the green grass under the saucepan lid had turned a murky shade of yellow.

Suspicious, Darshan took a spoonful of the pulao and threw it to some crows that were scavenging for food nearby. Hungry, they swarmed upon the rice in a moment, gobbling it up – and then one by one they fell down, dead.

'Heaven be praised,' exclaimed Darshan, 'for saving me from death!'

He threw the remaining pulao into the sea and returned to the old woman's house, hungry and worried that the prince and princess might have conspired together to attempt his murder.

That evening, when Kavin returned from his visit to the palace, he discovered Darshan sitting on the ground outside the old woman's house. He could tell immediately that something was wrong; Darshan was not his usual cheerful self, and instead stared into the distance, forlorn and depressed.

'My friend, what's wrong?' asked the prince. 'Have I neglected you? I'm sorry I've spent so much time in the company of the princess.'

Darshan could see that Kavin's concern was genuine, and realized his fears were unjustified. Kavin couldn't have played a part in the devilish plot of the poisoned pulao. Indeed, as much as he loved him, Darshan knew the prince probably wasn't clever enough to have hatched such an ingenious plan. So Darshan told him what had happened, revealing some of the pulao that he had kept as his evidence, saturated in poison and wrapped in a handkerchief.

'Who on earth could have done this to you?' said Kavin, horrified.

'Your betrothed,' Darshan revealed.

At first, the prince didn't want to believe him, but then he remembered that Darshan had never lied to him in the whole history of their friendship. Torn, he asked Darshan what he wanted to do. Together, they talked through the night, and Darshan explained his plan.

The next day, the prince followed Darshan's instructions. On his way to the palace, he gathered some snow, which he rubbed into his eyes as he approached the princess's chamber. The snow stung and tears began to stream down his face. As the princess came out to greet Kavin, she was surprised to find him looking so upset.

'Why are you crying, my love?' she asked.

'I'm grieving the loss of my friend,' the prince told her, acting as best he could to appear distraught. 'He died this morning without any explanation.'

Gulizar threw her arms around Kavin and hugged him, though not out of compassion but because she wanted to hide the enormous grin that had appeared on her face.

'Oh dear,' she said. 'How tragic.'

The prince pulled from his pocket a bottle of wine.

'I want to drink away my sorrows,' he said.

He led the princess to the balcony and for the rest of the afternoon they drank the wine. However, whenever the princess was not looking in his direction, Kavin poured out his cup into the garden below them. The bottle was soon empty, and the princess had consumed so much of it that she fell into a deep sleep.

As the princess slept, the prince began the second part of Darshan's plan. He crept to the gardener's hut and stole a shovel, which he then laid in the fire until it was hot. Carefully, he lifted the shovel from the embers and gently touched it against Gulizar's back, leaving a mark. Although the princess stirred, she did not wake.

Next, Kavin searched Gulizar's room for her pearl necklace, discovering it in the ivory box she had shown him at the lake. He then returned the shovel to the gardener's hut and went back to the old woman's cottage.

At midnight, Darshan and the prince sneaked out of the cottage and took their horses and belongings to a graveyard a mile away. Whilst the prince had been at the palace, Darshan had gone to the market to procure them disguises – Darshan was now dressed as a fakir, while Kavin wore rags and pretended to be his humble disciple. In the graveyard, they set up camp, and slept until daybreak.

In the morning, Gulizar rose from her sleep with the most terrible headache and a sharp pain on her back. She was dismayed to find her ivory box empty and discarded on the rug, her prized necklace stolen. She was so upset that she forgot the pain on her back, and hurried to her father to tell him about the robbery.

The king was extremely angry that a robber had managed to penetrate the walls of the palace, and scolded his guards. He issued an immediate warrant for the robber's arrest and the guards left the palace to search the city to find them.

A short time later, in the bazaar, Prince Kavin, still dressed in a poor man's clothing, was trying to sell the pearl necklace to a goldsmith.

'How much do you want?' the goldsmith asked.

'Fifty thousand rupees,' Kavin replied.

The goldsmith scoffed. Everyone knew that the king was looking for his daughter's pearls, and the goldsmith had immediately realized that the man before him must have stolen them.

'All right,' the goldsmith agreed. 'Wait here while I fetch the money.'

But, instead of returning with the gold, the goldsmith brought back two burly guards from the palace and the kotwal – the chief of police. They arrested Kavin and took the necklace from him.

'How did you get into the palace to rob the princess?' the kotwal demanded.

'I didn't,' said Kavin. 'I received that necklace from the fakir I serve as a disciple, and he told me to sell it for him.'

Angry, the kotwal ordered Kavin to lead him to the fakir. Together, they journeyed to the graveyard, where they found Darshan sitting by a fire, his eyes closed in prayer. Out of respect, the kotwal waited until the fakir had finished praying, then asked him how he had obtained the necklace.

'Tell the king to come here and I will tell him myself,' said Darshan, putting on the gravelly voice of an elderly man. The kotwal realized he had no choice and sent for the king himself.

Frustrated and angry, the king soon arrived at the graveyard in the company of his guards. But on seeing the fakir, who appeared so devout, he decided not to risk upsetting the heavens by accusing him. Instead, he politely asked him how he came to have the necklace.

'Last night, whilst we were praying here,' Darshan explained, 'we saw a terrifying thing – a ghoul.'

The hairs on the king's neck stood on end, and he shuddered. No ruler liked to hear of ghouls wandering their kingdom. The fakir continued:

'It was dressed in the finest clothes, like a princess. But as we hid and watched from behind a tomb, the ghoul dug up a body from its grave and began to eat it.'

The guards gasped. The king looked as though he might be sick. Darshan adjusted his hood and cleared his throat.

'I was angry,' he said, waving his stick in the air, 'so I chased it away, beating it with a shovel. While running away, the ghoul dropped a necklace, and that is how I found it. Now examine your daughter, and my story will prove true.'

The king summoned the princess and asked to look at her back. Gulizar lowered the back of her dress and there, upon her shoulder, was the mark of a shovel.

Heartbroken, the king turned to his guards and ordered them to take his daughter away and lock her in a cage for the rest of her days, which was the only way to protect the city from a ghoul. The princess fell to her knees.

'Please!' she cried. 'Have mercy, for I have committed no crime!'

But the king turned away as his guards began to

drag his daughter off. However, Darshan suddenly stood.

'Set her free!' he ordered. 'For we should forgive and forget.'

The king, who knew that the judgement of a wise old fakir must surely be respected, told his guards to do as the fakir said. As the guards cut Gulizar free from the ropes that bound her, Darshan and Kavin shed their disguises. The princess was relieved to see the prince, but shocked to see that Darshan was still alive.

Darshan approached her.

'Do you still think of me as a threat to be disposed of?' he asked. 'Did I not deserve mercy too?'

The princess wept, and bowed, pressing her forehead to his hand.

'I'm sorry,' she said, 'for you have saved me from imprisonment and now I see you are my greatest friend.'

Together, Darshan, Kavin and Gulizar returned to the palace with her father, where Darshan recounted the long story of their exile and adventure to the Ivory City. Learning how Kavin and Gulizar were betrothed, the king was very pleased, for he had long wished for his daughter to find a royal husband.

After a celebratory dinner, the king gifted Kavin and Darshan a number of wonderful things: two horses with ivory manes, six elephants, the most elegant new robes to wear, a dozen caskets of gleaming jewels and the camels they needed to carry them home. For surely the prince would now be welcomed back to his home country with his new wife, the fairy princess?

Of course, he was. Darshan and Prince Kavin made the long journey back to their homeland with Princess Gulizar and the riches with which they had been rewarded. Kavin's father was so proud to see him return with such a beautiful wife at his side, and the greatest treasures anyone had ever brought into his country, that he forgave his son.

The prince and the princess lived out the rest of their days in happiness and good health, and were beloved by their subjects, one day becoming king and queen themselves. And Darshan was there at their side until their final days – their chief vizier, and the man who loved them most.

A Princess and a Prince

Illustrated by

Sasha Staicu

On the shores of the Black Sea, there was once a great empire, ruled by a powerful emperor with a fearsome temper. With every year that passed, he extended his empire further and further into the continent, defeating any army that dared to fight back. Upon conquering these new lands, the emperor demanded that their defeated leaders send him their firstborn sons as hostages, so that none would be tempted to rebel against him.

One such ruler, King Ionuț, was not able to

fulfil the angry emperor's demands, for he had one daughter – Florina – but no sons. The king was worried that if he failed to send a son he might be branded a rebel, a charge punishable by death. His wife and daughter would likely suffer too, cast out into the streets to die in poverty, shame and misery.

Florina had noticed that her father had become sick with worry. He no longer smiled or hugged her. Instead, he spent his days in council with his advisors, his brow furrowed and his mouth curled into a frown, desperately attempting to find a way out of his dreadful predicament. As his sickness worsened, the king fell into a deep depression. Bed-bound and exhausted, the king anticipated that the emperor's order to end his life would arrive at any moment.

'Father,' asked his daughter, 'what can I do to help you? I will do anything you ask because I love you more than life itself.'

'You have been a very good daughter to me, but there is nothing you can do,' the king replied.

Florina listened, concerned and confused, as her father continued.

'We fought off the emperor for many, many years. But I can no longer fight as I did when I was a young man, in the days when our enemies feared me. My arms are weak, and I cannot brandish my heavy mace in battle. The stag roams free in the forest now, because he no longer fears my arrow. And the emperor will come for me, because I cannot send a son to him as hostage.'

Florina considered his words, and sat at her father's side. He looked so frail, and half the man she remembered him to be before the emperor had stolen their kingdom from them.

'Then let me go as the hostage,' she announced bravely.

The king sighed.

'No, little one,' he said. 'Who knows what dangers you would become entangled in if you embark upon this quest.'

Florina was headstrong, however, and once her heart was set on something there was little anyone could do to divert her from her goal.

'I may not be a prince,' she said, 'but am I not still the daughter of a great warrior and king?'

For the first time in many months, a smile appeared upon her father's face. He hugged her, full of pride.

'Then, so be it,' the king declared solemnly. 'Go and prepare for your departure.'

Florina was both excited and scared about the mission that lay ahead. She had long yearned to explore the world outside her country's borders. She gathered together some food and provisions for her journey, and picked out a sword to wield in combat. She borrowed some clothes belonging to the king's page, pulling on trousers and a shirt.

She washed her hair and cut it short. It became scruffy as it dried, sticking out in all directions, and it pleased her very much to run her fingers through it. And yet she still felt that she did not fit her new clothes quite right. So, taking some bandages, Florina wound them about her chest until it was flat. As she stood up straight and looked upon the mirror, a happiness warmed her heart unlike any other she'd felt before.

For a moment it was a shock that the princess had vanished. But when that surprise was over, she saw the boy stood in her place was not a stranger. It felt as though he'd always been in her life: a boy with whom she shared the deepest of secrets, a familiar old friend who had been with her as long as she could remember. For as long as *he* could remember.

'From now on,' he said aloud, 'I shall be Florin.'

Florin headed to the palace stables to choose a horse to accompany him on his journey. He passed by the gallant stallions and the majestic mares, his favour falling upon an old, lame warhorse that rested on the straw in the corner. Gently, Florin combed its matted mane, at which the horse began to speak:

'Master, are you the son of the king whom I once carried into battle? The prince?'

Florin was surprised that the horse had spoken but pleased that he had called him a prince.

'I am,' he said, and it felt so right to say so.

'Then take me as your steed,' the horse declared. 'My name is Cosmin, and if you tend to me for ten days, a lame horse I'll no longer be.'

Florin accepted Cosmin's proposal, and for the next ten days he cared for him. He was a rather demanding creature (he wished to be washed morning and night, and due to his teeth being broken he would only eat barley boiled in milk), but Florin persisted, and his hard work paid off. For, when ten days had passed, Florin entered the stable to find that the warhorse had become strong again, his coat as glossy as satin.

The horse thanked Florin and said, 'You have made my life worth living, and now I will obey your every wish. Let's depart for the emperor's capital. And as I served your father I will serve as your counsel too.'

Florin agreed, and bade his father and mother farewell. Mounting Cosmin, he sped away from the palace and into the unknown.

After a few days of travelling through the forest, they came upon a bridge of brass. As they prepared to cross it, a wolf appeared, blocking their path. Its teeth were bared, its body arched to pounce. Its tongue flared like a firebrand, and Florin trembled with fear.

But the young prince knew that, should he turn back, his family would be in danger of the emperor's wrath. And so, with every fibre of his being, he drew upon the courage in his heart.

Galloping forward, he raised his sword, and fixed his gaze upon the wolf's yellow eyes. The second before they collided, the wolf panicked and darted away, allowing Florin and Cosmin to reach the other side. Turning his head to watch the wolf disappear into the distance behind them, Florin and Cosmin cantered onwards.

They soon came to another bridge, this time made of silver. Upon it stood a lion that roared so loudly the young prince worried his ears would bleed. But he knew that, should he turn back now, his family would suffer still. And so again he drew courage, raised his sword and fixed his gaze upon the lion's orange eyes. As Florin galloped towards it, the lion jumped aside, and once again they passed in safety as the beast fled into the woods.

A little later, they came to another bridge, this one made of gold. From below it rose the thorny head of a dragon, its body covered in scales.

Florin knew that, should he turn back now, he would always live in shame of his cowardice. So, for a third time he raised his sword, and fixed his gaze upon the dragon's green eyes. Faced with Florin's charge, the dragon flew away. Relieved, Florin hoped that there would be no more bridges in their path.

Soon they had travelled so far that Florin's kingdom was left far behind. On their journey they passed waterfalls and meadows, where flowers Florin had never seen before grew wild, and the song of the chaffinch pleased their ears with its sweet melodies. Florin longed to swim amongst the water lilies in the crystal waters of the lakes, or to rest below the blossoming trees.

'A knight only rests when the battle has ended,' the old warhorse reminded him, and Florin reluctantly agreed. He knew that he must not be distracted from his promise to the king, and, despite his growing tiredness, went on his way.

As their adventure continued, Florin and Cosmin encountered many more trials, and all sorts of magical spirits that sought to trick them into leaving their path. But they faced every challenge, and Florin, much like his father before him, became a skilled warrior.

One day they saw a lock of golden hair upon the road in front of them. Florin's eyes narrowed as he considered it, wary of another trap.

'Should I pick it up or leave it behind?' he asked the wise warhorse.

'If you leave it,' Cosmin advised, 'you will regret it. But the same can be said if you take it too.'

Florin rolled his eyes, for Cosmin, he had come to understand, had a curious way of answering his questions.

'Then I will pick it up,' Florin said with a sigh, and did so, before mounting his horse again.

He tucked the golden hair into his shirt, and rode on, drawing ever closer to the emperor's capital. Over hill and down dale, by day and night, they travelled, and finally, caked in mud and sweat, arrived at their destination.

***

The emperor's palace was the most enormous building upon which Florin had ever set eyes. Its bricks were black as coal, and the foreboding atmosphere of the city surrounding it made the young prince grip his steed's mane more tightly than before. As they walked through the streets, many children ran alongside them, begging for money. By the time they reached the palace gates, Florin had given all their remaining food away.

'I am Florin, the son of King Ionuț,' he declared to the emperor's guards, 'and I offer myself here as hostage.'

They bound him with ropes, and Florin looked at Cosmin sadly as he was steered away to the stables.

One of the guards gave him a hard shove, and Florin obediently entered the palace. As they walked through the corridors, Florin stared at the many paintings of the emperor: a shrewd-faced man with greying hair, his stare cold and calculating.

The guards led Florin to a dormitory and pushed him inside. The door slammed behind him, and he heard a *click* as he was locked inside. Slowly, the scared faces of many boys emerged from the shadows.

Later, Florin was taken to the emperor's throne room. In person, he was just as his portraits had depicted, if not even more fearsome. Florin was not permitted to speak in front of his new master and stood silent as the emperor considered him. The emperor grinned, seemingly delighted to add another hostage prince to his collection. But something about Florin seemed particularly special, and so the emperor announced that he wished for the prince to serve him as his page.

Florin was a hard worker, and threw himself into his duties. Though carrying firewood to and fro was exhausting, he loved that the chore made him feel strong. He busied himself helping the imperial chefs prepare meals, adding a number of delicious dishes he'd learned to cook during his travels to the emperor's capital. However, as the emperor began to praise Florin for his talents, the other hostage princes grew jealous that the newest arrival had earned their master's favour.

They taunted and teased him, but Florin knew how to deflect their cruelty with his good humour and clever wit, and soon the boys accepted him as a friend. Florin grew to love the time they spent together in their dormitory: the jokes and conversations they shared, and the games they played. In a place that was meant to be a prison he somehow felt free.

Early one morning, the boys awoke, and one

of them gasped, pointing to the floor beside Florin's bed.

'Look!' the boy cried, waking the other princes. 'Florin just dropped a lock of golden hair!'

Florin saw that the lock he had picked up on his journey had indeed slipped from his shirt.

'His heart is sworn to another!' said a second prince. 'Oh, brother, tell us who she is!'

The princes gathered around Florin expectantly, and he smiled. On his travels he had heard a ballad, sung by many throughout the lands, about a beautiful princess: Iliane of the Golden Tresses. And so, clearing his throat, he sang of Iliane and her long blonde hair, who had a beauty like no other. When he finished, the princes erupted in cheers, firing questions at Florin.

'Did you meet her?'

'Did you kiss her?'

'Is she as beautiful as they say?'

After that, the princes asked Florin to tell them

more stories about Iliane every night. And so, each evening, he created new tales, which he would sing until they fell asleep.

Soon, however, the stories had spread throughout the palace, from the princes to the guards to the cooks to the pages and the handmaids and, finally, to the emperor himself. Annoyed that his favourite prince had not shared the tale with him, the emperor summoned Florin before his throne. He demanded to be shown the lock of hair, and Florin placed it in his hand. The emperor curled the soft lock round his finger and grinned gleefully.

'You will bring me the girl whose lock of hair is twisted in my palm,' he growled, 'or I'll cut your head clean off. Go, take your horse and find her.'

Florin nodded, excited to be freed from the palace walls, though terrified by the emperor's threat. He hurried towards the door, but, just as he reached it, the emperor called out to him: 'Be warned: should you not return, the heads of all the princes here will roll into the gutters – and the fault will be yours.'

Florin gulped. He knew the emperor meant what he said, so he hurried to the stables, where Cosmin was glad to see him after so much time apart.

'Do not be afraid, master,' he consoled the worried prince. 'Only last night I dreamt of the princess whose lock of hair you found. She has long been trapped on a distant isle, but I think I know the way.'

Florin returned to the emperor and asked him for a ship to travel to Iliane's location, and treasure to tempt her to return with him. The cunning emperor admired the strategy and agreed to his request. By nightfall, Florin and the warhorse found themselves at sea, a new quest ahead of them.

***

After seven weeks at sea, the winds aiding their journey, the ship finally arrived. Stepping ashore, Florin gazed up at the sky. Revolving above the island, through some sorcery, high up in the clouds, were three castles.

The hot sand burned Florin's feet, so he opened the casket that stored the emperor's treasure and put on a pair of slippers he had found amongst the loot. They were embroidered with fine silk, and studded with precious gems and pearls.

As Florin and Cosmin advanced towards the castles, they saw a figure descending from one of them on a staircase. Her golden hair flowed behind her, and Florin instantly recognized her as Iliane, the princess from the song. Reaching the ground, she began to walk towards them, and Florin bowed. As he rose, he saw that she was as beautiful as people said … and she was smiling at him. The princess had seen the stranger from her window in the castle, and immediately thought him handsome.

'What beautiful slippers,' she said, admiring them. 'Are you a merchant, visiting our shores to sell goods like these?'

'I am indeed, Your Highness,' said Florin, beaming. 'And upon our ship are many other treasures, should you wish to see them.'

The princess looked back nervously at the castles in the sky and then to the ship.

'I cannot be gone for long,' she whispered, 'for I am the captive of a genie and I do not wish to anger him.'

'Then come but for a short while,' Florian encouraged her, 'and you will be home in no time.'

The princess agreed and followed them aboard the ship, where Florin laid out for her a table of treasures in the cabin. Dazzled by the items on display, the princess picked up each and every one.

But as the princess lost herself in examination of the exquisite craftsmanship, Florin secretly set sail, and when she climbed back up to the decks Iliane was shocked to find herself at sea, with the island and its castles far behind them. She began to panic and considered jumping overboard, but Florin soothed her.

'We offer you safe passage from the genie who imprisoned you,' he said, 'to the land of a great emperor, which you can call your home.'

'The emperor?' Iliane grimaced. 'It's from him that I fled in the first place when he stole my father's kingdom. From one prison you take me to another. Quite the knight you are . . .'

Florin turned to Cosmin, confused, as the princess marched off, annoyed. For the rest of the journey, she refused to speak to him, and hid away in her cabin instead.

As the ship approached the emperor's kingdom, storm clouds gathered overhead. Thunder sounded across the bay, and lightning ripped through the sails. Florin persuaded the princess to finally come out of her cabin, and together they joined his crew in a small boat.

The warhorse swam, pulling the boat by a rope tied to his harness. Navigating the rising tides, they made it to shore. Yet as soon as they had touched land, Iliane gasped and pointed to the cliffs, upon which stood a witch whom she recognized as the mother of the genie they had just escaped.

'Oh, please don't let her take me back to him,' she cried, and Florin hugged her close.

He leapt on to Cosmin, and helped Iliane up on to the warhorse's back. With the princess gripping his waist, they began to ride.

'Faster!' Florin cried, as he looked over his shoulder, alarmed to see the witch following them at speed on a broomstick. Cackling, she raised her hands to the sky, commanding for more lightning to fall upon them. The princess screamed as one bolt scorched her shoulders.

But the old warhorse had seen many witches in his long life and knew just what to do about them. So, as he galloped on like a hurricane, he told the prince and princess what they should do.

Obeying Cosmin's instructions, Iliane reached into the horse's ear and pulled out a whetstone, which she cast on the road behind her. As soon as it hit the ground, it transformed into an enormous mountain that stretched so high it blocked the witch's flight.

But the mountain did not stop the witch for long. She climbed over it and was soon pursuing them once more. So, again the princess reached into Cosmin's ear, this time removing a brush. She cast it behind her, and a forest grew from its wooden handle, so fast that in only seconds it had spread for miles and miles. Its branches and vines twisted together so tightly that not even a deer could have penetrated it.

However, the witch was not daunted, and still

she followed, tearing through the forest with her sharp talons and haunting them with her screams.

In desperation, Iliane took a ring from her finger that she had not wished to lose. She threw it to the ground behind them, and from it rose a tower, as hard as steel and gleaming like a mirror, into which the witch flew. Falling to the earth, the witch was caught upon the tower's sharp turrets. Enraged, she started to breathe fire, which set the tower alight. And as it fell, so did the witch, now a lifeless body in the rubble.

Arriving at the emperor's palace, Florin turned to the princess and bowed his head in shame.

'It's true that I deceived you,' he said solemnly. 'For to save my head, and others' too, I brought you here at the command of the emperor. I am not a merchant but a prince and, just like you, I am a prisoner.'

Florin was scared to look at Iliane, lest he be met with disappointment in her eyes. In the silence, he longed for her to say something, but instead she took his hand.

'Then we ought to come up with an escape plan.' She smiled, and led him towards the palace gates and the guards that awaited their return.

***

Princess Iliane had been held captive by enough odious men in her life to know what was ahead of her. Just as she predicted, as soon as the emperor saw her beauty, he demanded that she marry him and spend the rest of her days as his wife. But Iliane saw a different destiny for herself, and so, in order to delay the hasty wedding preparations, the princess decided to set an impossible task that she hoped would send the emperor mad.

'I can only marry you,' she lied, 'if you gift to me for our betrothal the vase of holy water that is guarded in the chapel near the River Jordan.'

The emperor was so enchanted by Iliane that he wished to find her any object she might desire. Though he was too lazy, of course, to do so himself. In his place, he summoned Florin, who had so successfully delivered the princess to him and proved himself worthy of the most complicated missions.

Florin was worried to be called before the emperor again, but pleased for the opportunity to see Iliane. Most of the time, they were separated, stealing only glimpses of each other at dinner, when Florin served the emperor and the princess their food. But, although they could not speak, they did not need words to express how they felt, and it was clear in the smiles they shared that both were deeply in love.

As he stood before the emperor, Florin barely listened to his words, his focus drifting to Iliane instead, memorizing each line of her face and the locks of golden hair that fell down across her forehead, just in case it was the last time he laid his eyes upon them.

'Go, Prince Charming,' roared the emperor, interrupting Florin's daydreams. 'And do not loiter on the way, or your head will roll. As will those of your fellow princes if you dare to flee.'

Heartbroken to leave Iliane, Florin reluctantly set off on his way.

The vase of holy water was guarded by an order of nuns, in a chapel deep in the desert. The nuns never left the vase unattended, taking turns to watch over it every hour of the day. The only time it was left alone was once a week, during the visit of a holy hermit with whom the nuns would sit in the sun whilst he preached.

Upon finally reaching the chapel after many weeks' travel, Florin and Cosmin discovered that the hermit had just arrived there too. Excitedly, the nuns poured outside and took their seats beside him, offering the hermit food and water in exchange for his wisdom.

As the nuns listened, Florin tiptoed into the chapel as quietly as a cat. He grabbed the vase from the altar and ran outside where the warhorse patiently waited. Florin seized his mane, and they fled through the desert. But, spotting the vase in Florin's hand, the nuns raised the alarm, and fell to their knees in prayer. Angry, their friend the hermit stood, and stretched his arms to heaven:

'Lord, my Lord, three times holy, grant that the rascal who has lifted a sacrilegious hand against thy vase of holy water may be punished! If he be a woman, be he now a man. And if he be a man, be he now a woman.'

From the clouds above came a blinding light, and Florin covered his eyes. He feared he'd fall, as he felt a tremor run through his body. A searing pain ran across his chest, and he struggled to breathe. He knew that he'd been cursed, but was not sure exactly how.

When they were far enough from the chapel to be safe, Florin drew the warhorse to the river. There, other young people had gathered, for the day was hot. Happily they bathed in the cool water, and from a distance Florin watched them enviously.

'Why are you sad?' asked Cosmin as he drank from the river.

'Because I wish to sit here as they do, no shirt upon my back.'

'Then do so,' said Cosmin. 'For one person's curse is another's blessing.'

Confused, Florin slowly removed his shirt and unbound the bandages it concealed. Beneath, he found his body changed, his chest as flat as the other boys around him. Florin was so happy that he danced in the river, making splashes and laughing with joy.

Returning to the emperor's palace, the prince marched to the throne room where he presented the vase of holy water to his master.

'All-powerful Emperor, I salute you!' Florin cried. 'I have fulfilled your mission, and I hope you have no more need of me. May you be happy and reign in peace.'

'Prince Charming,' said the emperor, 'you have proved yourself like no other prince in my care. And so I choose you to be my successor when the time comes for my death.'

Florin realized then that the emperor had stolen the princes of so many lands because he had no rightful heir of his own. But, despite this, Florin's heart fell at the thought of Iliane being forced to marry the emperor, and the long life they would share.

However, while Florin had been away hunting for the vase, Princess Iliane had had enough time to devise a plan. Upon Florin's return, she had

'Why are you sad?' asked Cosmin as he drank from the river.
'One person's curse is another's blessing.'

instructed that a bath be filled with mare's milk and heated.

'My dear emperor,' she said as he handed her the vase, 'let us bathe together. For soon we will be married, and I'm so thankful for this gift.'

Excited, the emperor hurried to his chambers, where he found the bath waiting, stripped off his clothes, and jumped in with a splash. But the princess had ordered that the milk be heated hotter than a furnace, and into it the emperor disappeared without a trace.

As word spread of their ruler's death, the people of the many kingdoms over which the emperor had tyrannized celebrated with joy. Florin and Iliane married, and feasts were held in their honour for three days after. Florin became emperor of the city and all its lands, and Iliane his empress with the golden tresses.

And perhaps they still rule there to this day.

The Dog and the Sailor

Illustrated by

Pete Jordi Wood

Once upon a time, there was a kingdom that basked in the heat of the tropical sun. The king was kind and compassionate, the land was full of laughter, and everyone was happy. Everyone, that is, but one . . .

The young witch Valéria was talented and powerful, but very, very lonely. In a land with no troubles, there is little need for magic, and so nobody sought out Valéria or her spells. Valéria was envious of the king and his family, popular in their glorious palace. And so she made a plan.

She first cast a spell on her purse, granting herself all the riches her heart desired. And then she cast another spell on herself, becoming the most beautiful person in the world.

The palace guards were bewitched by Valéria's beauty, falling under her control. They instantly followed her command to take her inside. When the king saw Valéria's beauty, he too fell under her spell – and Valéria took over the palace.

Before long, the whole kingdom bowed to Valéria. But Valéria was not content, for nobody truly loved her. She still felt alone, and she grew more and more bitter.

One day, Valéria noticed a young boy fleeing from the palace with her enchanted purse. He had stolen it! She called out, expecting him to be bewitched by her beauty, but he resisted the magic.

Valéria was furious, and in her rage she cast a spell that turned the boy into a puppy, with a lion's tail and webbed feet like a duck. Still overcome with fury, she transformed everyone else in the kingdom into beasts and birds.

One by one, they lost their human forms, becoming winged creatures and wild beasts. Skin became fur, hands became claws, and soon all that could be heard from the palace was the shrill orchestra of birdsong, the chattering of chimpanzees and the howling of wild dogs and wolves.

Finally Valéria summoned up a mighty wave that submerged the kingdom beneath the sea. As the kingdom sank, the puppy kicked his webbed feet and swam against the tide of the witch's magic, far enough away to escape . . .

* * *

Some years later, in England, a bright but restless boy called Ruan lived alone with his mother on the coast of Cornwall.

Every day he would walk to the port and watch the sailors come and go from their ships. Some of them had grown very rich on their adventures, returning to build large, impressive houses that dwarfed Ruan's tiny cottage. Ruan was envious, longing to be a sailor too and to live a life less ordinary, travelling the high seas and making his fortune.

However, Ruan's mother feared losing him to the waves and so she forbade him from going to sea. The family was very poor, and even though Ruan's mother worked day and night to provide for them, they continued to struggle. So, with a heavy heart, Ruan agreed to begin an apprenticeship with a tailor and contribute a little money of his own.

Ruan was soon miserable! He hated standing still all day as the tailor pinned fabric to him like a dummy. He fidgeted so much that the tailor grew impatient and dismissed him. Returning to his mother with no money, Ruan begged her to let him go to sea. His mother knew he would never be happy unless he followed his heart, and eventually she agreed to let him go.

Ruan headed to the port where he found a job as a cabin boy. At last he was free to leave his dull life behind and set off on an adventure! But being at sea was much less fun than Ruan had expected. He hated scrubbing the decks, and was often caught by the captain talking or lazing in the sun instead of working. As months, and then years, passed by, Ruan grew frustrated that he was still a poorly paid cabin boy. But the captain refused to make him a sailor until he'd shown he could be more responsible.

Then tragedy struck. One night, Ruan was meant to be on watch, but fell asleep. The ship hit a reef and sank, and the crew perished. Only Ruan survived. Clinging to the wreckage, he was carried by the tide to the coast of a foreign land.

There he was cast ashore, his clothes torn to rags.

Ruan couldn't speak the language and found it impossible to find a job on another ship. He was forced to beg for food, but few showed him generosity or kindness. As the winter nights grew longer and colder, Ruan headed to the quay and stared out on to the dark waves. Just as he thought all hope was lost, something appeared in the water.

It was a dog, swimming towards the shore. Ruan ran down to the beach to greet the creature as it emerged from the sea. The dog shook its tail in delight. Soft black curls coated its body, and Ruan recognized that it was a water dog, like those he had sometimes seen working on fishermen's boats.

The dog was so affectionate and playful that for a moment Ruan forgot his sadness. And then, to Ruan's astonishment, the dog spoke!

'Don't despair,' the dog said. 'There's still so much in this life for you to do.'

The dog had been carrying a purse between its teeth, and now dropped it at Ruan's sandy feet. The dog told Ruan to look in the purse, and to wish for his heart's desire.

Ruan couldn't believe his eyes or his ears, but he did as the dog instructed, reaching into the purse. When he drew out his hand, it was filled with gold coins!

Still in a state of disbelief, Ruan thanked the dog and waved as it ran down the beach and disappeared back into the sea. Shaking his head, Ruan walked to the town – this handful of gold would change everything.

In the weeks that followed, Ruan lived life to excess. He stayed in the fanciest hotels, ate the finest food and wore the most elegant clothes. His new wealth attracted attention, and some people saw an opportunity to exploit his generosity.

The dog told Ruan to look in the purse, and to wish for his heart's desire.

But when the money ran out Ruan's new friends disappeared too.

Alone once again, Ruan returned to the quay and stared into the watery darkness. And, once again, the dog appeared and told him to check the purse.

Ruan did as the dog said, discovering more gold inside. However, this time the dog asked Ruan to use the money to do a favour for him in return – to build a ship and assemble a crew.

***

It took many weeks, but at last the ship was ready and they set sail. Ruan and the dog were careful to hide the dog's magical powers from discovery, but one day a cat overheard them talking secretly. This was not just any old cat but one of Valéria's servants – a spy!

The cat went immediately to its mistress and

told her what it had seen. Valéria had been hunting for the dog for many, many years. Enraged, she conjured up a mighty sea monster, hungry for the ship and its crew.

As the monster drew near, the dog joined the crew to fight it. But Ruan was terrified. He remembered the terrible night that he lost his first crew. He cowered below deck, paralysed by the fear that history would repeat itself.

The ship was enveloped in fog and angry clouds. Ruan heard the dog barking and the roar of the sea monster as it circled the ship. The hull creaked and groaned so much that Ruan feared the ship would split in two. The noise continued all night until the sun rose, and the monster retreated.

Emerging from the hold, Ruan discovered the dog badly injured. Retrieving the witch's purse, he closed his eyes and made a wish – a wish so great it used up the last of the purse's magic.

Reaching inside, Ruan withdrew a vial full of a

sparkling lilac potion. He rubbed the potion into the dog's wounds, and his cuts and bruises disappeared. Returned to full health, the dog thanked Ruan for saving his life.

'But I hid like a coward,' said Ruan, full of guilt, 'when you were so very brave.'

'I haven't always been brave,' said the dog. And he told Ruan his story: how his kingdom had fallen under a witch's spell, and how he had run away. He told Ruan how his heart's desire was to return to the kingdom, to become human again and to somehow save his people, now turned into animals and living beneath the sea.

Ruan smiled.

'Then I will help you.'

***

The next day, the dog and the sailor rowed away from the ship together. When the dog gave the word, they sat on the side of their little boat and then fell backwards into the sea.

The pair swam down into the depths, until they reached a vast meadow. Ruan found he could stand, as if on land, and breathe, as though the water were air. Together, he and the dog began to walk towards a castle in the distance. Inquisitive creatures looked on from their hiding places, curious about their secret kingdom's uninvited guests.

'Welcome!' said Valéria as Ruan entered the palace. 'I have been expecting you.'

Ruan recognized that Valéria was very beautiful, but he was able to resist her charms.

'This dog claims you used magic to take this kingdom as your own,' said Ruan. 'Turn him back into a human and undo your spell!'

'I will turn this dog into a human again,' said Valéria. 'And I will give you half this kingdom. We will live in this beautiful palace together, forever – if you will be my husband.'

But Ruan shook his head. He didn't want the witch, nor her wealth, nor her palace beneath the sea.

'You can have anything you want! Just tell me your heart's desire,' pleaded Valéria.

'My heart's only desire is to help my friend,' said Ruan.

'I order you to be my husband,' Valéria shouted.

'No,' Ruan replied.

It was a word the witch had not heard in a very long time. It left Ruan's mouth like a bullet that shot to her heart.

A blinding burst of colours filled the room, as if a rainbow had pierced the darkness of the palace. The guards awoke from their enchantment, for the power of that one word had broken the witch's hold over them, and they turned their weapons on Valéria.

But the dog stood in their way and turned to the witch.

'What does *your* heart truly desire?' he said.

Valéria was surprised; no one had asked her that question before. After a long pause, she answered: 'To be needed – as I once was when people asked me to make potions to help them.'

'Good,' said the dog, 'because you are needed now. You are the only person who can help us. Please undo your enchantments.'

Ruan watched in awe as Valéria reversed her magic, and all the animals in her underwater realm turned back into human form: the fish became fisherfolk, the birds and beasts became villagers and townspeople. The waves drew back, and the kingdom rose up to the surface of the sea, right next to Ruan's ship.

Ruan stared at the dog in amazement. Beams of light radiated from his body, and the dog returned to his original form as the king's son, Nikolai – now grown into a handsome prince.

At the prince's request, the king pardoned Valéria for her crimes, provided that she promise to use her magic only to help others in future. Valéria asked Ruan to show her the purse. She waved her wand over it, and its magic returned. Everyone agreed that Ruan should keep the purse as a reward for his part in saving the kingdom, and the king invited him to stay with them to rule at Prince Nikolai's side.

Ruan really wanted to stay. He loved the prince, but he couldn't leave his mother alone in poverty. And so Prince Nikolai and Ruan sadly parted, and Ruan made the long voyage back to England to find his mother.

Ruan's mother was certain that her son had been lost at sea, so she was overjoyed at his return. But when Ruan told her the story of his adventures, she was horrified.

'You left behind a kind and handsome prince – what were you thinking?' she cried. Picking up the magic purse, she reached inside and closed her eyes.

When she withdrew her hand, a beautiful gold ring sat on her palm. 'Go back at once and find him,' she said, giving Ruan the ring.

And so, with his mother's blessing, that's exactly what Ruan did. Leaving the magic purse with her, so that she would have all the money she would ever need, he sailed back to his prince, and they agreed to get married, for they were truly in love.

The couple called on Valéria's magic to conjure up the perfect wedding celebration, whisking Ruan's mother from across the sea to join the festivities. Valéria was overjoyed to use her powers for good at last. The entire kingdom rejoiced to see happiness return to the land, and Ruan and Nikolai lived happily ever after.

ABOUT THE TALES

Researching this book

There are numerous challenges in presenting old folk tales to modern readers. As folk stories have their origins in the spoken word, their structure can sometimes feel chaotic or repetitive when written down. Some use language that we now recognize as racist, homophobic or misogynistic. In addition, folk and fairy tales were not always meant for children, and many feature adult themes. In assembling this anthology, therefore, it was necessary to adapt these stories to make them more suitable for younger readers.

Folklorists use a catalogue that lists the world's folklore called the Aarne–Thompson–Uther Index or 'ATU' for short. In the ATU, similar tales are grouped together as 'tale-types' – stories that share plots and common motifs. Where a story has been assigned an ATU tale-type, I have listed that in this appendix.

One such tale-type – number 514 in the ATU – is known as the 'Shift of Sex', and is an example of what we might refer to as an LGBTQ+ tale-type. Stories from this tale-type exist around the world, dating back to the original Sanskrit texts of India's *Mahābhārata* as well as the Middle East's *One Thousand and One Nights*. A common motif in these stories is that the protagonist is transformed, usually through an act of magic, from one sex to another. But while this tale-type is in some ways an excellent starting point for anyone looking to delve deeper into LGBTQ+ folklore, it also illustrates how the process of adapting tales is not without its complications.

On the one hand, it is extremely exciting to find many centuries-old stories in which characters who are assigned one gender at birth transition into another and find happiness in doing so. On the other, examples of this tale-type usually imply that a person can only belong to a specific gender identity if they possess the physical characteristics conventionally associated with that gender.

Even the name of this tale-type – the 'Shift of Sex' – is potentially problematic. To many people who identify as trans or non-binary, this preoccupation with our physical appearance and bodies is offensive and objectifying. To make matters worse, this tale-type usually relies on the awkward 'gender reveal' trope to create tension and dramatic effect.

Trans men are men. Trans women are women. I therefore made the decision in my adaptations of stories belonging to this tale-type to remove gender reveal tropes and, rather than focusing solely on the transformation of bodies through magic, instead to highlight the journey of the characters from gender dysphoria to gender euphoria – and hope.

'The Girl in the Market'

Adapted from 'Eine schlüpfrige Geschichte' in Afrikanische Legenden, *Carl Einstein, 1925.*

Essentially, this is the tale that inspired me to create this anthology. Dausi is such an important character – a trans woman of colour who becomes a queen. I hope the rediscovery of this tale leads to future research into Dausi's incredible story, and proves that more stories about characters like her must surely exist, just waiting to be reinterpreted and retold.

This story is adapted from an original tale collected from Benin, formerly known as the Dahomey Kingdom. That original is possibly a variant of the 'Shift of Sex' tale-type and, if so, is certainly a very rare example in which a character assigned male at birth is transformed into a woman. In my adaptation, rather than experience a physical transformation after ingesting a cassava root, Dausi undergoes a magical and spiritual transformation at the hands of Death and the spirits of the savannah instead. She is given an ending in which she has truly come to love herself and reached a level of happiness with her own identity that she's never experienced before.

'Double-Flower Temple'

Adapted from 'Double-Flower Temple' in Master Not Discuss (Zi Bu Yu)*, Yuan Mei, 1788.*

The wonderful and cheeky Yuan Mei was a story collector long before Europeans had even coined a term for folklore studies. His observations of the society of eighteenth-century China – which were not only groundbreaking but also very brave – make him a hugely significant LGBTQ+ ally in history.

He was never afraid to tackle taboo subjects, recording stories of LGBTQ+ characters with heart and humour.

This story is adapted from a lesser-known tale from Yuan Mei's work that I hope will delight the LGBTQ+ community – gay ghosts being queer activists are awesome! Although LGBTQ+ characters do sometimes die in folk tales, this tale features a couple who return to haunt their persecutors and, in so doing, change society for the better. In my version I wanted to stress the inspirational and eternal nature of the love between the heroes, and how that lives on in the minds and attitudes of the community they leave behind.

Note for researchers: Paolo Santangelo published an excellent and exhaustive English-language version of the Zi Bu Yu *called* Zibuyu, What the Master Would Not Discuss. *It is an incredible work of translation that includes hundreds of Yuan Mei's poems and stories, but it isn't suitable for young readers.*

'The Falcon in the Garden'

Adapted from 'Vasilisa the Priest's Daughter' in Russian Fairy Tales (Narodnye russkie skazki), *Aleksandr Afanas'ev, 1855–1863.*

Originating from Russia, this story (ATU tale-type 884B*) is – like all these tales – open to readings from many different perspectives: some people might connect to Vasily as a feminist icon; others, as a gender-fluid warrior.

I wanted to include a tale about gender that featured a protagonist whose story isn't preoccupied with dysphoria or the physical traits of their body, but instead focuses on them being unashamedly euphoric throughout. Although the original Russian fairy tale also veers towards the discomforting 'gender reveal' trope, I love how Vasily sidesteps this narrative beat before it lands, and uses it to hold a mirror up to the austere King Barkhat, exposing him for the person he truly is.

As a non-binary person, I also wanted to showcase a character who demonstrates the autonomy to flex their pronouns as they wish, and Vasily's change throughout. I hope readers will agree that whatever his, her or their gender identity is, it cannot be disputed that Vasily is a wise and kick-ass hero to be remembered.

'The Spinners and the Sorcerer'

Adapted from 'Jean-Parle' in Contes Populaires Canadiens, *Charles Marius Barbeau (*The Journal of American Folklore, *Vol. XXIX), 1916, and 'Fitcher's Bird' in* Children's and Household Tales (Kinder- und Hausmärchen), *the Brothers Grimm, 1812–1857.*

There are many examples of this story from around the world, similar to the famous story of Bluebeard, and this tale might be considered a variant of ATU tale-type 311, 'Rescue by the Sister'. Sisterhood has long been linked to themes of queerness in feminist writings and queer studies.

This adaptation is a hybrid of the Brothers Grimm version and a Canadian variant recited by Narcisse Thiboutot in 1915, at Sainte-Anne-de-la-Pocatière, Kamouraska, Canada. Barbeau tells us that Thiboutot learned this tale from the late Charles Francœur about six years previously. I wanted to adapt this tale because of its extraordinary closing scene, in which the heroine literally burns to the ground the patriarchy, systemic oppression and the concept of a heteronormative wedding ceremony. It's a powerful message: three 'spinsters' – women typically regarded as unworthy of love – choose each other over a relationship with a man.

Note for researchers: check out the works of Pauline Greenhill, who has written in depth about this tale-type, and Angela Carter, whose collection of retellings of folk tales, The Bloody Chamber, *includes her own adaptation of this story.*

'Marco and the Mountain of Gold'

Adapted from 'The Princess who Groans: Man or Woman?' in Folk-Lore from the Cape Verde Islands (Part I), *Elsie Clews Parsons, 1923.*

I grew up in a Catholic family and when I first read Marco's story it immediately resonated with me – and surprised me! Not only was it refreshing to see a religious icon from Christianity like St Peter come to the aid of an LGBTQ+ character, but I found Marco to be a hero unlike any other I had seen – a person who defies gender binaries and class conventions, overcomes discrimination and hate, and ends up marrying a princess as accepting of unconventional attitudes as he is. However, the original version of this tale was problematic; it featured discriminatory language and included both a gender reveal storyline and a body transformation.

I have chosen to adapt this story in a way that preserves some of the positive traits of the original folk tale but removes the emphasis on Marco's physical transformation. Marco is a character on the fringes, an impoverished outcast deemed 'lesser than' by others. But in living unapologetically as his true self he ultimately finds happiness, adventure, love and gender euphoria without the need for physical transformation. Instead, it is the attitudes of those around him that are forced to transform, when a person they look up to and revere – St Peter – declares that Marco is a man and the prince the kingdom needs, in an exquisite mic drop.

'The Tale of the Rabbit God'

Adapted from 'The Tale of the Rabbit God' in Master Not Discuss (Zi Bu Yu), *Yuan Mei, 1788.*

Another classic from Yuan Mei's collection, this is essentially a ghost story that blurs the line between folklore and Chinese mythology. To this day, you can visit the Rabbit God temple in Taipei and make an offering to Tu'er Shen (literally translated as 'Rabbit Deity'). It is one of the few surviving, active religious shrines in the world dedicated to a gay god – if not the only one. The original tale comes from Fujian province in China.

'The Soldier and the Peasant'

Adapted from 'The Grave Mound' in Children's and Household Tales (Kinder- und Hausmärchen), *the Brothers Grimm, 1812–1857.*

I grew up reading fairy tales by the Brothers Grimm, but even when I was very young, this story struck me as distinct from the others. Sometimes a story just feels queer, even if queerness is not explicitly mentioned. Featuring two male characters who walk off into the sunset (or, in this case, sunrise) having promised to support one another and live together, 'The Grave

Mound' achieved something extraordinary, becoming a story that found its way into popular nineteenth-century literature whilst featuring a same-sex couple.

Note for researchers: have a look at Elliot Gordon Mercer's essay 'The Grave Mound: a queer adaptation' in Transgressive Tales: Queering the Grimms *(edited by Kay Turner and Pauline Greenhill).*

'The Ivory City'

Adapted from 'The Ivory City and its Fairy Princess' in Indian Folk Tales, *Joseph Jacobs, 1892.*

Just as themes of sisterhood as subtext for sexuality are explored in 'The Spinners and the Sorcerer', 'The Ivory City' explores themes of brotherhood in much the same way. This story is based upon a delightful fairy tale from India that explores unrequited love, jealousy and devotion, in which the 'LGBTQ+

sidekick' trope is turned on its head. The prince's loyal companion – who explicitly states his love for him on numerous occasions – gets to take centre stage as an intelligent and adorable lead.

I was so happy to find this story whilst reading Jacobs' collection and it was one of my favourites to adapt, but I have not been able to source any academic writings about it. I hope that it will be investigated in more depth in the future as it really deserves to be.

'A Princess and a Prince'

Adapted from 'Ileana Simziana' in Legende sau basmele românilor, *Petre Ispirescu, 1872.*

This Romanian tale is another example of the 'Shift of Sex' tale-type and has striking similarities to the story of Mulan. Unlike the version of that story made famous by its two Disney adaptations, the fairy tale on which this version is based features a magical physical transformation of the protagonist from a binary 'female' to a binary 'male' at the story's conclusion. Once again, this shift is extremely jarring for trans and non-binary readers when presented in this way.

In my version, I wrote Florin as a representation of some trans and non-binary people in our community who experience feelings of misalignment between their gender identity and their bodies. However, I wanted Florin's tale to reflect that gender euphoria is something often experienced throughout the lives of trans or non-binary people in myriad different ways.

Florin specifically experiences discomfort and anxiety surrounding his breasts, which can only partially be relieved through binding. Through the magical 'curse' at the story's conclusion, Florin's chest is transformed into a more conventionally masculine form, allowing him to feel a sense of gender euphoria when he relaxes topless for the first time at the river. But although this physical transformation contributes to Florin's overall sense of gender euphoria, it is not the only factor. Florin experiences gender euphoria throughout his adventure, in moments in his everyday life in which he feels symmetry between his gender expression and his gender identity, such as the scene in which the other princes accept him as their brother.

Note for researchers: check out the works of Psyche Z. Ready, who has researched many different variants of tale-type 514.

'The Dog and the Sailor'

Adapted from 'David Husmandssøn' in Danske Folkeæventyr, *Jens Kamp, 1879.*

Previously listed in the former index as 'The Dog in the Sea', this tale-type was renamed in the current ATU as 'The Dog and the Sailor' (tale-type 540).

My adaptation of the story is based on a variant from Denmark by Jens Kamp, although a line from the original folk tale suggests that the sailor in the story comes from England (the country he 'returns' to at the end of his adventure), which is where I've placed him in my version. The motif of a black dog with a curly coat – likely a Portuguese water dog – recurs in variants throughout Europe, and suggests that the story possibly originates from Portugal, where water dogs – and tales of them saving sailors' lives – were common throughout the Algarve, where they worked on fishermen's boats.

The antagonist in this story – a witch whose power over others is her attractiveness – is a really interesting foil for an LGBTQ+ hero. Because he can defy the witch's power, the sailor can be read as having a number of queer identities, but in my adaptation I have positioned the story as a gay romance.

In the original, the sailor rejects the offer of marriage to the prince in order to return home to the parents he abandoned in poverty with the riches they need to survive. It's a moving story about a man who sacrifices his one chance to live a life filled with love in a community that accepts him for who he is, to care for his elderly parents far away: the culmination of a character arc that sees him grow from a selfish child to a selfless adult.

The story originates from a period in which it was the responsibility of a child to care for their parents when they were no longer able to work. For many, this is still a reality today. As the only child of a disabled parent, it resonated deeply with me.

I believe that folklore – the transition of our stories from one person, one generation, to the next – is, by its very nature, destined to change. And so in this version I have honoured the original storyline in which the sailor selflessly returns to his mother, and yet, with her blessing, is able to marry his handsome prince too. My version is a little kinder to the witch, offering her a redemptive arc in which her magic is the means by which the sailor is able to bring his mother to join them, allowing him to continue to support her, but to live in a place where he is accepted for who he is, loving the man he wants to love.

Fairy tales, after all, live beyond our ordinary world, in a place where all our wishes can – and do – come true.

ACKNOWLEDGEMENTS

Creating this anthology would not have been possible without the help of many brilliant people, the majority of whom – from editorial to design – are LGBTQ+.

I want to thank my amazing mum who has always believed in me and has encouraged me to pursue a career as a writer . . . even when the rejection letters piled high and my dreams seemed out of reach. Thank you, Mum, for teaching me to never give up.

Thank you to the illustrators, Anshika Khullar,

Ez Silva, Harry Woodgate, Jenn So, Mario Hounkanrin, Nontira Kigle, Sasha Staicu, Sophia Watts, Xin Tang and Zat Vornik, for making this book so beautiful and for bringing each of these tales to life. You are all so amazing, and it has been such an honour to work with you. Thank you, especially, Sophia Watts, our wonderful book designer, who has worked tirelessly to build a talented illustration team from around the globe that is predominantly LGBTQ+.

Thank you to our authenticity readers, Amy Derickson, Anni Domingo, Justin Ho, Jay Hulme, Helen Gould, Hamza Jahanzeb, Al MacKay, Ravi Teixeira, and others who did not wish to be named, whose careful scrutiny of the anthology through its development helped us shape it into this book. Thank you for your honesty and insight, and for helping us figure out how to take often problematic stories and re-envisage them for a contemporary world.

I want to thank Ben Horslen, my awesome editor, for making this journey an amazing, creative and positive experience that I will never forget. Thank you for being so kind and patient and smart and wise, and for caring about this book as much as I do. Thanks also to the editorial team, Wendy Shakespeare and Josh Benn, Sarah Maclean in Marketing and Sarah Doyle in PR, and Kelly Hurst for including this title in the Puffin Classics collection and honouring LGBTQ+ folklore in such a beautiful way. Thank you, Emma Jones, Joe Marriott and the Penguin WriteNow scheme, for finding me, championing me and changing my life for the better.

Thank you, Dino Fetscher and Joe Dines, for believing in this project from the start and helping me to share these special stories with the world. Thank you, Claire Wilson at Rogers, Coleridge and White, Giles Smart at United Agents, and Michelle Kroes and Lindsey Bender at CAA, for helping me to sell this book to publishers and producers when others were resistant to take it on. Thank you so much for believing in me and my work. Thank you to Freddy Wexler and your team, and Emma Burge and Maor Azran, for your encouragement and wisdom.

Thank you to the folklorists who came before me – the boots on the ground who travelled the world in search of these tales and were the first to write them down. Without you we would never have been able to create this anthology. Thank you to the scholars who have dared to research queer folklore when no one else would. Most of all, thank you to the storytellers of the past . . . the ordinary folk, unnamed and uncredited, who told these stories on their journeys and helped spread them across the continents; thank you for preserving our collective LGBTQ+ history.

Finally, thank you to my friends – my chosen family – for rooting for me every step of the way. I love and appreciate you so much.

ABOUT THE AUTHOR

Pete Jordi Wood (he/him) is an author, illustrator and screenwriter from Cornwall, who writes and creates art from a queer perspective. Pete has written original drama for the BBC and Channel 4, and now writes and illustrates books for children and adults. He describes himself as a 'fairy tale detective' and has dedicated himself to the academic study of queer folk tales, myths and legends.

ABOUT THE ILLUSTRATORS

Anshika Khullar

Anshika Khullar is an Indian, non-binary, transgender creative with a BA in English Literature and Media from the University of Brighton. They have a focused interest in intersectional feminist narratives, a study which has invariably informed their art practice, with illustrations that are colourful and detail-oriented, and which often tackle overarching socio-political themes.

Ez Silva

Ez Silva is a Rotterdam-based contemporary artist. In her art she expresses her fascination with the female form and explores the many facets of femininity in an Art Deco/Art Nouveau-like style.

Ez grew up in Cabo Verde with seven brothers and sisters. When she was eight, her family moved to Rotterdam. Growing up in a big family as the youngest of her siblings, she developed a strong and versatile character. She is determined and creative, meticulous and a perfectionist, all of which is reflected in her artwork.

Every drawing has its own unique story, and it is through this form of storytelling that Ez communicates with and relates to her audience. Her drawings deal with questions about identity, femininity, strength and vulnerability. For women, it is easy to relate to the female subjects in Ez's work and reflect on one's own experience as a woman. The women in her drawings express joy, sadness, passion, pain, lust, beauty, comfort, recognition, shame, love or disgust, and one cannot help but be moved in the same way. Ez's artwork is all about finding out who she is as a woman, who she wants to be and how she wants to express herself as an artist to the world.

From Ez: In my teenage years I started dating guys. I soon realized I had this strange feeling about girls. I could not really understand what it was. At the age of twenty-five I met this girl who was on a university trip to China, as I was. Then it finally happened – I kissed a girl for the first time. I'd never felt so liberated. We kissed on the dance floor in a club in Shanghai. It was magical. But, unfortunately, I wasn't ready for it then. But ten years later, I was done hiding my true colours. I came out as gay. I wish I had done it sooner!

Harry Woodgate

Harry Woodgate (they/them) is an award-winning author and illustrator who has worked with clients including National Book Tokens, Google, the *Sunday Times Magazine*, HarperCollins, Simon & Schuster, Walker Books, Andersen Press, Bloomsbury, the *Washington Post* and Penguin Random House.

Their books include *Grandad's Camper*, *Timid*, *Little Glow*, *Shine Like the Stars*, *My First Baking Book* and *The Very Merry Murder Club*.

Grandad's Camper, their debut author-illustrator title, won the Waterstones Children's Book Prize Best Illustrated Book 2022 and a Stonewall Book Award Honor from the American Library Association. It was also shortlisted for the inaugural Polari Children's and YA Prize 2022 and nominated for the CILIP Yoto Kate Greenaway Award, and was well reviewed by *Kirkus Reviews*, *School Library Journal*, the

Bookseller, the *Guardian*, *The Times Literary Supplement* and many others.

Harry is passionate about writing and illustrating diverse, inclusive stories that inspire children to be inquisitive, creative, kind and proud of what makes them unique.

Jenn So

Jenn So is a Chinese-Canadian illustrator who loves art, games, music and animation. Movies and TV shows, games and other various forms of pop culture often take a focus in and inspire much of her work. She also loves fantasy, magic, space and nature, and enjoys working these elements into her illustrations.

One of the nicest things Jenn has found about making art has been the ability to connect with others creatively. She's always striving to improve her skills in art, but being able to create what she enjoys while sharing in similar interests with her fellow artistic peers, writers and creators is one of the things she loves most about being an artist.

Jenn studied at the Ontario College of Art & Design and graduated with a BDes in Illustration, and she is currently working as a freelance illustrator and commission artist, while selling her art and running her online stores.

Mario Hounkanrin (aka Mariosupa)

Mario Hounkanrin is an artist, illustrator, designer, capoeirista and father based in Amsterdam, the Netherlands. He was born in 1978 in Cotonou, Benin and raised in Paris, France. He has had a passion for drawing since he can remember. Whilst studying science at Université Descartes (Paris), Mario decided to combine his two passions – visual expression and computer science – and became a graphic designer.

From 2001 until 2004, he worked for French *ELLE* magazine. Wanting to focus more on his personal artistic development, he became a freelance designer in 2004. One year later, NOMOON came into being, a creative agency Mario set up with college friends Camille Ouanounou, Julien Reynaud and Côme de Selva. For over ten years, NOMOON created websites, illustrations, and motion and graphic designs for renowned brands and communication agencies, such as Chanel, Kenzo, Diesel and BETC.

In 2014, Mario moved to Amsterdam. He currently entwines his graphic arts with his African roots, creating compelling illustrations that 'pair a minimal colour palette with shape design' (*Scene360* magazine), whilst critically addressing the position of the black body in contemporary culture. As Mario states: 'African arts and cultures are often overlooked or ignored. I wish to show how rich and inspiring they are.'

Nontira Kigle

Nontira Kigle is a queer graphic designer and illustrator with Thai roots, and lives and works in Augsburg, Germany. She has been self-employed since 2010 and designs for municipal institutions, publishers, theatre ensembles and organizations such as the CSD Augsburg. Since 2021, Nontira also started to draw queer illustrations, one of which even ended up in *Sinister Wisdom*'s 2022 calendar. In addition to her main work, Nontira also draws comic strips, which she uses to process everyday experiences, including homophobia. When Nontira is not sitting at the drawing table, she loves to play ukulele, organizes exhibitions and is involved with the lesbian community L*-AUX and the Dyke* March Aux.

Sasha Staicu

Sasha Staicu is a queer Romanian artist based in Glasgow. She makes short comics about imaginary characters loosely inspired by real life, designs album covers and posters for people she admires and is learning to tattoo.

From Sasha: I am a queer comix artist from Romania whose attention is monopolized by unorthodox ethnographies, discarded utopias, everyday disposable graphics and visuals that endure a long time. I currently live in a crypt in Glasgow where I am building a dream machine that will remove every curse in the world. Somehow.

Sophia Watts

Sophia Watts (she/her) is a queer, London-based designer/illustrator from Nottingham. After graduating from Leeds Arts University with a degree in Illustration, she began working as a children's book designer for Penguin Random House UK in the Puffin 6+ team. She has designed books for well-known authors such as Jacqueline

Wilson and Roald Dahl, as well as illustrating where she can on titles, such as the Puffin Clothbound Classics series. Sophia likes to work on projects that can inspire and educate the younger generation.

Xin Tang

Xin Tang (唐歆) is a New York-based, Chinese-American illustrator. They studied at the Fashion Institute of Technology in New York and tap into their Chinese-American heritage to inform their art. They use their art to explore and learn about their own heritage as much as they use it to share with others. Having grown up in the suburbs, they were simultaneously disconnected from their Chinese heritage and yet distinctly Chinese when around other people. Their unique perspective has informed much of how they view forms and colours in art, as well as gender in the context of themself.

They are often found using art to communicate to all kinds of people, and exploring the deep sense of feeling 'in between' in many different ways – in between genders, cultures, phases of life – and that is reflected in their use of mixed media as well. They value balance and fluidity in life as well as art.

Zat Vornik

Zat Vornik is an artist and illustrator from Moscow, Russia. After graduating from HITR Television School he begun working as a cinema and advertising storyboard illustrator, later expanding his practice further to editorial illustration, animation and printmaking. In his artistic practice, he explores the themes of the gay body, emotions and everyday life, creating surreal and vivid images with clean and realistic linear drawing. Born in Russia in 1992, he has had to deal with anti-LGBTQ+ discourse from the government and has opposed its dehumanizing effect by creating images of queer people as human beings living their life – sometimes spiritual and sometimes very mundane. As an illustrator, he likes to be a part of projects of cultural impact. One such project involves studying and reclaiming gay sexuality in Russia before and after the Bolshevik Revolution – and revealing that Russia wasn't always a homophobic country.